A Woman Like That

MARY LAY

Contents

Prologue

A s is often the case when an elderly aunt or great aunt dies, younger members of the family are tasked with clearing out the residence and disposing of the contents. So it was when Laura Merton, nee Curtly, passed away peacefully at her home in 1987. She had survived her husband Clive by three years, and had led a happy, if somewhat unusual life.

They had no children. This was not a great discomfort to them, as they had many other distractions and had bred Airedale Terriers for many years. It did however mean that the clearance and disposal duties fell to Laura's nephew and niece. They had not been a close family. Clive's sister had moved to Norfolk after the war, marrying a man who had investments in turkey farming and mustard. They prospered and raised their children, Michael and Lucinda in relative affluence, but had no interest in Laura and Clive beyond the ritual Christmas card complete with a summary of the children's activities and achievements that year.

Laura and Clive had travelled. Clive's job with the Foreign Office had taken them to many varied and exotic locations, living for two or three years in one place before moving on to the next. The war had been an exciting, exhilarating, and often terrifying time for them both. While Clive diplomatically negotiated on behalf of the British Government, Laura documented the surroundings she found herself in, always with an eye on the man (or woman) in the street going about his (or her) daily business and largely oblivious to the movements of nation states and their armies. She took up photography, kept up with her shorthand, and typed long into many nights with her dogs at her feet.

Laura's body of work was not recognised until late in her lifetime. Clive always referred to it as her hobby; one of the few things that Laura found annoying about her husband. She submitted articles to newspapers and magazines, with some small success. She published two short accounts of her time in Kenya and Ceylon, complete with her own photographs, which only had one edition of each printed and never caused any ripples in the *London Evening Standard*.

It was only shortly before her sixty-third birthday, at a party for one of Clive's friends who had been successfully elected to the local council, that Laura got chatting to a lecturer in social studies from one of the provincial universities. They exchanged contact details and over the following few months, Laura and the professor collaborated on a series of articles using more of her photographs, which were published by an international journal. Laura, having never wanted fame, declined the offers spawned from the articles to attend various symposia and lecture tours, and settled for the royalty cheques and a flurry of letters from admirers of her work.

Laura had kept all of her notebooks, her typed manuscripts and essays, and her photographs in well-labelled boxes in the attic of their final home in Oxfordshire. Michael and Lucinda, keen to sell the house and share the proceeds, stayed on after Laura's funeral to begin their exploration of the contents. They went from room to room, picking out various items that they wanted to keep, and others that would be removed and auctioned separately before the clearance company swept away the rest. Not for Michael or Lucinda the taxidermy from Africa, the brightly painted wall plaques from Peru or the six dinner services, one of which had twenty place settings.

On the second day, Michael left Lucinda examining books in the study and pulled down the ladder that led up through the first-floor ceiling to the attic. Clive had thoughtfully installed electric lighting and with a flick of a switch, Michael could see at least another two- or three-days' worth of items to be sorted through. He let out a sigh, which dislodged a plume of dust from the top of an ancient side table. It was lucky he owned his own business and wouldn't have to beg for more time off. Surveying the scene, he spotted a chair that looked like it could take his weight without collapsing, eased himself through the hatch and began lifting the lids on the assortment of crates and boxes.

Lucinda found him two hours later when she poked her head through the hatch, engrossed in a document and surrounded by note-books and piles of photographs.

"I've pulled out the first editions and a few novels signed by the authors. Everything else is so old or specialist, I doubt we'd get much separately for them. Are you ready for lunch?"

"Good Lord, have I been up here that long? Yes, look, grab a couple of those will you and take them down for me. Just be careful on that ladder. I'll bring these too, and I'll show you while we eat."

Lucinda wiped her fingers on a sheet of kitchen roll before picking up one of the black and white images on the kitchen table.

"So, they're not worth anything?"

"I shouldn't think so, not in financial terms. But it's the historical significance that's of value here."

"Can't we just leave them for the clearance people? I've got enough boxes of old photographs at home as it is from when we were kids. I really don't need any more and I doubt Evelyn will either."

"It's not always about the money, Luce. These things are important. Didn't you hear on Radio Norwich a while ago that the museum service was asking people, older people, to go in and record their memories? People live much faster lives now, and it's important that the next generation have first-hand accounts of how things used to be."

"I don't see what Norwich Museum would want with these though."

Michael drained his plastic camping mug of tea. His sister could be hard work at times. "These don't relate to Norwich, no. But they do relate to Reading, and there are other boxes with interviews Laura carried out in Swansea and Banbury. Those are just the ones I've looked at so far. I'm going to contact those museums and see if they want these for their archives. If they say no, then we can ditch them, but I want to make sure before they end up in a landfill somewhere, OK? Evelyn will only have to suffer them for a couple of weeks at most, I'm sure."

Laura's plan

"Mother, Father, I have decided what I want to do with my life." Laura had put down her knife and fork on the dining room table and sat with her hands clasped in her lap.

Her parents exchanged glances. This was not the first time Laura had announced such a decision. Some weeks before, it had been an archaeologist. A month before that, a zookeeper. Her mother continued with her lunch. Her father swallowed, placed his cutlery onto his plate and dabbed his mouth with his napkin.

"And what have you decided?" He asked the fourteen-year-old apple of his eye.

"A lady policeman."

Jonathan Curtly smiled benevolently at his daughter.

"Now Laura, you know that women cannot be police constables. It is a job for a man. Women become teachers or nurses, or sometimes secretaries, and then they get married like your mother did and they raise a family."

"But I want to be a lady policeman. I could be the first one!"

"I really don't think so. It is not a suitable occupation for a young woman. Finish your lunch."

Laura had made up her mind and a little disapproval from her Father wouldn't dislodge her conviction. At fourteen she knew she wanted to make the world a better place, catch miscreants and lock them away so good people could sleep safe in their beds. At least that's how the newspapers described the work of the police. She had wondered over the past few days while her decision was forming, why there never seemed to be any lady police constables mentioned in the newspapers. They didn't appear in the novels she had been reading recently either, and one would think if they did exist, Mrs Christie or Mrs Sayers would have written about them. The Chief Inspector was always a man, she realised now, as was the Sergeant, and the Constable. Laura would change all that. Laura would be the first.

Laura was not the first. Indeed, Jonathan Curtly had been misinformed about the ability of women to join a police force. Though most did not have the authority to arrest criminals, women were being employed across England by various forces, principally to work with vulnerable women and children. However, policing was still very much seen as a job for men.

When Laura mentioned it to her school mistress the following week, in the hope of learning how one might go about being the first woman to do something, she was surprised and disheartened at the reply she received.

"Why on earth would you want to do something as dangerous as that?!"

"Oh, but I don't think it would be all that dangerous, Miss Collins. I imagine it would involve mostly walking around with my hands clasped like so, and asking little boys why they weren't in school." Laura enacted her fantasy while she spoke, with her hands behind her back and a stern, serious look on her face.

"It's no place for a woman, you mark my words young lady. The Lord made men and women different for a reason, and why any lady would want to put herself in with criminals and the like I don't know, I'm sure. There's something not right about it. Not right at all. Not ladylike."

"But it could be, Miss Colins. Wasn't there a time when women couldn't be doctors? Or teachers?"

"Well, yes but those are different. And I can't say that women doctors are as good as men in any case. Women should be nurses or midwives, they've no need to be doctors. And as for teachers, women like me teach girls like you and sometimes the babies, and men like your father teach the boys. It's how it's always been."

"Don't you want to teach boys?"

"Good heavens no. I wouldn't know where to start! No, women do women's jobs and men do men's jobs and the sooner you put that idea out of your mind the better. Now, show me your needlework."

The answer was similar from everyone Laura raised the subject with. No one thought that a woman should want to become a police constable, let alone that there should be a force willing to employ them. The same objections were raised time and again; it was too dangerous, women wouldn't be able to run fast enough or climb over walls, women wouldn't be able to remember all of the laws, women should be at home raising a family.

Laura was fortunate that she did not have to seek employment as soon as her schooling ended. Her father was a headmaster at a boys' school, and though she had been a disappointment as far as her sex, Laura was his pride and joy and certainly not required to contribute to the family finances. Laura's mother made efforts to introduce her to local families who in time would have eligible bachelors, with a view to a reasonably long engagement. While Laura was comfortable, and occasionally helped at her old school with the younger girls, she was also bored. She emersed herself in novels, amply supplied by Mrs Christie and others, in which Laura assumed the role of Marple (or sometimes, Poirot) and tried to solve the case before the final chapter.

The round of county balls and fundraisers to which her mother insisted she attend, opened Laura's eyes to more of the situations faced by the public at large. By listening to polite conversation, and asking a question here and there, Laura began to understand that there were more ways in which a person could help their community than simply rounding up criminals. She still harboured a dream of being a policewoman, but slowly she began to wonder if a career might be found in the modern science of social work.

Once again, when she broached the subject with her parents two or three years later, their reaction was less than encouraging. Raising money for the poor and needy was one thing (and a very worthy and dutiful thing) but associating with them, engaging with them in their own habitat, was quite another. Unthinkable, pronounced Laura's mother. Unsuitable, declared her father. It would damage the reputation of the school and could influence the Board of Governors when Jonathan Curtly's terms of employment were next reviewed. Laura was forbidden from consorting with the lower classes for anything other than activities which required service of some kind.

Laura was still stubbornly clinging to the thought of a career as a social worker when she met Clive Merton at a charity dance in aid of the local dispensary. Clive had been dragged along by a sister of a friend, Rose, as her escort and had then been stationed at the bar while Rose danced the evening away with a number of different men. It was just as well that Clive had Laura to gaze at across the ballroom floor. He would never admit to it being love at first sight, but he was very much interested. Laura had not wanted to attend the ball, and certainly not with her mother as chaperone. She was now twenty-one years old and considered around the county to be quite the catch if anyone was brave enough to try and land her.

Clive made inquiries. Towards the end of the evening, he asked Laura to dance. Mrs Curtly hardly disguised her delight, and almost shoved Laura into Clive's arms as the band began a waltz. They continued with a second waltz, during which Laura learned that Clive had recently started a job with the government and hoped to work his way into the Diplomatic Service. Still bored, and a little dizzy, Laura returned to her mother and bid farewell to Clive for the evening.

Laura's mother made her own inquiries, which encouraged her to extend an invitation to Clive to join them for dinner some weeks later. Laura too had been investigating, though in her case, the subject was a course offered at Birmingham University which gave the graduates a certificate in Social Work after one year of successful study. It was open to women, and Laura wanted to enrol. She could not do so without her father's permission or funds, and this would again be a problem for her.

Jonathan flatly refused. He was becoming exasperated by his daughter's outlandish requests and welcomed his wife's information on Clive Merton and his prospects. The sooner Jonathan could marry Laura off, the better it would be for everyone he decided.

Laid on her bed, collecting her thoughts after a fit of tears prompted by her father's latest dismissal, Laura rolled onto her side and stared vacantly at her dressing table. A pile of novels beckoned her. She got up, and as she was about to take the top book from the pile, she glanced at the newspaper she had been reading that morning. A small advertisement drew her attention. It was for a correspondence course claiming to provide the student with all the investigative techniques required to embark on a career of journalism. With her hand on the top book's cover, Laura had an idea.

***

"You hope to join the Diplomatic Corps, Mr Merton?" Laura's mother knew the answer but was skilled in polite dinner table conversation.

Clive was positioned opposite Laura at the dining table with Mrs Curtly's friends. Jemima Grosvenor was to his left, with Dr Gideon Grosvenor to Laura's right. Clive had been surprised but pleased to receive the invitation and was very much enjoying his view of Laura.

"I do yes, perhaps in two or three years. One has to wait for the right opportunity of course, but I have it on good authority that I am the type of man they look out for."

"Laura is going to be a novelist, aren't you dear," Mrs Curtly prompted.

"Mother, it may not lead to novels. I could become a poet or even a playwright." Laura smiled sweetly to the assembled company.

"I don't think I would have the imagination for that," stated Jemima.

Laura silently agreed with her. "Do you read, Mr Merton?"

"A little, yes, mostly the classics, Dickens, Shakespeare, Homer, that sort of thing. I rarely have time these days to dive into a good book. Have you begun a manuscript, Miss Curtly?"

"I have begun a correspondence course. It is to last a year, and I shall receive a set of assignments to complete along with a reading list. I'm really rather excited about it." Laura's smile was genuine.

She had told only a small white lie to her father about the correspondence course. Instinctively she had known that journalism would provoke the same reaction in him that policing and social work had done. But creative writing, that was surely a profession suitable for a young woman. There were certainly many advertisements for those courses in the newspapers and magazines, and she wouldn't have to go away to the likes of Birmingham to study. Jonathan Curtly was relieved that finally his daughter was exhibiting some level of sensibility, and eagerly made out a cheque to the A. N. Corley Writing School to cover Laura's tuition. He was so relieved, he did not think to do his own research into the type of courses they offered.

When the time approached for Laura's final assignment to begin, she was faced with a problem. How to find a suitable subject to interview without raising the suspicions of her parents too soon. Laura knew she must tell them eventually, as the lack of literary output could only be excused for so long by saying she was not ready to share her work publicly. It was while Laura's mother was entertaining her old friend Lucy Worthington for lunch one day that Laura found her opportunity.

"Of course, that was when I was working in the munitions factory, during the war. We all had to do our bit. I met some intriguing characters there, but I wasn't sorry to get married to Charles and leave of course." Lucy Worthington helped herself to another small sandwich triangle.

"Did you say a munitions factory, Mrs Worthington?" Laura asked.

"Yes, dear. Most of the girls there were younger than I was, and I worked in the kitchens and not on the factory floor. But one or two of the women I do still keep in touch with. One or two others, not of our class you understand, I keep up to date with through acquaintances."

Laura studied her teacup for a moment and then looked up at Lucy Worthington. "Do you think, Mrs Worthington, that I might be able to speak to one of those women? You see, I have to write an ... essay for the correspondence course I have been enrolled on this year, and I think talking to someone completely different might give me some ideas of interest to my tutor."

"Laura is going to be a novelist," beamed Laura's mother.

"I can certainly make some inquiries. It was a long time ago, and the women have spread out across the capitol now."

"Not to the lower boroughs, surely?" Laura's mother's smile had been replaced by a look of concern for her daughter's safety.

"One or two, but let me see what I can arrange. When does this essay need to be completed, Laura?"

"I have another six weeks. I'm sure it won't take me long to write it once I have some good material to work with."

"I do have one person in mind. She was always jolly good fun, but rather a closed book when it came to her past. Perhaps you could find out something of her background."

Laura nodded slowly. Investigating the past of a stranger was exactly what she had been hoping for.

London, 1933

Dear Mr Corley,

Please find enclosed the first draft of my final submission for your review. I am most grateful that you have agreed to read through it before I go too far, as I am still unsure whether this is a suitable subject.

I first met Mrs Hawkins some weeks ago, after being given her address by an acquaintance. I was hoping to write a piece about overcrowding at the turn of the century. However, Mrs Hawkins is such a character, and had so very much to say, that I began to feel as if it would be churlish to leave out anything she had told me. I hope to offer this series of interviews then, as conducted by myself over the course of several weeks. I have not yet been able to verify any of the details shared with me. My notes and comments are included throughout suffixed by 'L.C.'.

Yours sincerely

Laura Curtly, Miss

Interview 1.

[I asked Mrs Hawkins to introduce herself, and to start at the beginning, as far back as she could remember. L.C.]

My name is Harriet Hawkins. I have had other names, but that's the one I was born with and the one I've always liked the best. I don't know why you want to know about my life, it's no different to so many others, but as I have nothing else to do today, I will tell you. It was very nice to hear from Lucy Worthington again, or Lucy Parks as I knew her at first before she got married, it's been a while since I last saw her. She was a good friend, but I'm sure we'll get to that eventually.

Are you sure you want to do this here? It's a bit noisy, that's all. I'm used to noise, but with you being a writer and all, I thought you might want somewhere a bit quieter than a Corner House. Thank you for the tea, make sure you write that down, that I said thank you. I don't want anyone thinking I'm on the scrounge. Though it wouldn't be the first time if they did. Anyway, do you want me to start? Make good notes, mind! I shan't be saying it all twice over.

My parents, George and Emma, moved to Reading from Thatcham in Berkshire two or three years before my sister Rosina was born. Yes, a bit of a fancy name. My mother was rather a fancy woman, there was a bit of the gypsy in her, people said. I couldn't say for sure though. She had dark hair and Rosina got that from her. I never did. I had my father's hair and eyes and ... well, you can say 'stockiness'. I'll agree to that. Rosina was two years older than me. I remember she was always twirling around and dancing. I can't say how many times she was warned not to do that. Father said it a lot, but I don't remember Mother saying it. If you want to know, Mother wasn't always as strict with us as Father was, and I don't remember her telling us off much. Even when she did, she never tanned our hides.

My first memory? Now you're asking. Let me see... I remember sitting on our doorstep looking out at the court. Not a court with judges and all that; Reading had lots of courts, courtyards I suppose, back then especially around St Mary's Butts and St Giles. You'll have to stop me and get me to explain things if you don't understand, I won't mind, but I forget that you young people don't know how Reading used to be. It's changed so much since I was a girl. Anyway, it must have been West Court because we lived there first at number four and then after the fire, we moved to number nineteen.

[Reading is a large town in Berkshire, England. Its principal industries being biscuit baking and the brewing of beer. A number of notable Quaker families are memorialised throughout the town in parks, gardens and schools. L.C.]

Number four was near the entrance to the court, and we'd have everyone coming and going past our door. A lot of them would stop and pass the time of day with Mother, and at night they would bang on our door if they were looking for someone. Father hated that. Father hated being woken up when he was sleeping. He worked hard, Father did, mainly labouring on the railway or sometimes at the tin factory. He never earned much, that's why we lived in the court. I remember there were cobbles and a gutter along the middle of them that everyone would throw their rubbish into. Not just rubbish, if you understand me, the chamber pots were emptied into it every morning as well. A man would come and sweep it every few days but in summer it smelled bad.

Inside we had two rooms just for us and then there was a space to cook and have a wash at the front that we shared with the nine other families in the building. I'd say go and have a look, but the corporation pulled them all down a while ago. As far as I know there aren't any courts left in the Butts now. I don't think you can imagine what they were like if you'd never lived in one. You writers all come from better places than the likes of me. When I say we had two rooms, one was a bedroom with two beds and a tiny space between them just big enough to stand up in if you were sideways. There was a small window that wouldn't open. It wouldn't have looked out on anything pretty if it had, just an alley and the back of the next court. Yes, we had bed bugs because everyone had bed bugs. Everyone in the courts anyway.

The other room Mother called the parlour. That was her putting on airs. It was the room with the fireplace. I do remember we got so cold in winters there, Father took the bedroom door off its hinges and burned it one year when he'd had no work on account of the frozen ground. The window in the parlour was a bit bigger than the bedroom one, but it had the same view and if it hadn't been nailed shut it would have fallen out of its casing. Everything rattled when the trams were running. Mother and Father had their chairs, and me and Rosina sat on the floor. There was a sort of sideboard against one wall where Mother and Father kept our plates and cutlery and a few other bits and bobs.

Clothes? We only had what we wore. I wore what Rosina was too big for and she wore what Minnie Draper upstairs had grown out of. Minnie would have had her older sister Alice's cast offs, and I doubt Alice ever got anything new. Father had two shirts and two pairs of trousers that Mother would wash out every two or three days in summer but only once a week in winter. Then she'd use the water we'd all had a bath in to save on the soap. I hated that scummy bath, I can tell you. I'd have rather stayed dirty for a month than get in that water every Saturday night.

But we were lucky you know, to have two rooms. Some of those buildings in the courts had two families in the same space that we had, and those families weren't small either. I don't know why Mother never had any more children after me, perhaps I was what people call a difficult birth, or perhaps she found ways to not have any more. I'll not say any more about that, so don't ask me. Perhaps it was because of what happened to Rosina. This tea is good, isn't it, a proper strong brew.

We went to school of course. We went to the Neale's School behind St Mary's church. Father was strict about us going and he'd be angry with Mother if she didn't send us. We had morning lessons and then we'd be sent home for lunch, but we didn't always have lunch. A bit of bread and dripping most days, perhaps an apple or pear if we could slip one off a market stall on our way home. Looking back, I suppose it all got a bit easier after Rosina died.

I will tell you about her now, but I wanted you to understand first how we were all living on top of each other. There have been times in my life when I'd have given my own teeth to have two rooms like we did in the courts again, but no one would ever say they liked living there. No one was clean. No one had any money – if they did, they moved out sharpish!

Rosina was about seven and I was five. It was at the end of January and Father was working so we had money for coal. I remember that. I don't remember where he was working at the time, but to have coal and not to be sent out to find scrap wood to burn, that was a rarity, so I remember it. Rosina had a new red frock, one of Minnie's. It was too big for her, but Mother wouldn't turn any of them down, because we'd grow into them eventually.

We'd had our dinner and Mother was in the front washing up the plates. She couldn't have been gone more than a couple of minutes. I was sat on Father's chair with my legs swinging because it was as big as a throne to me then. We could, you know, when he was at work. Rosina was dancing around the room like she always did, with some tune or other in her head. The grown-ups afterwards all said she must have tripped on the rug. I don't know, I don't remember everything, but I remember her scream. She fell into the fire.

[Mrs Hawkins took out a handkerchief at this point and dabbed her eyes, although I don't think she was actually crying. I think it was for the look of the thing. L.C.]

I don't think I moved. I think I must have been too scared to do anything. Mother came tearing in, her hands all wet. She got Rosina on the floor and rolled her up in the rug. Mother was shouting all the time. I can see it now, as if it were just yesterday. Mother got burnt a bit herself, but Rosina was black and red all down her front. Her hair was mostly gone. I remember she looked so strange without her long hair. And the smell! Have you ever smelled burnt hair or skin? No, I don't suppose you have. It stays with you.

Mrs Draper came in and sent Minnie off to find Father. She and Mother took Rosina into the bedroom, and then Mrs Draper came and took me up to her room. I wasn't allowed back into our rooms for days, I had to sleep with Minnie and Alice, and walk back and forth to school with Minnie every day. I know now of course that Rosina died two days after the accident. Such a terrible way to go, and she was so young.

When I was allowed to go back to Mother and Father, our things had been moved over to number nineteen. All except the rug of course, and Rosina. I didn't like it at number nineteen. It was at the far end of the court, and we had a room on the top floor. Father put up a curtain so that we had somewhere to sleep, but the big bed that Rosina and me had slept in wasn't there and I just had a mattress on the floor with some blankets. We didn't have people banging on the front door all night at number nineteen, but it was a noisy building. Mr and Mrs Arnold in the room next to us were old; he never went out and she would drag a basket up and down those stairs two or three times a day, as old as she was. But he would shout! Gawd, he would rant and rave at her almost every night. Father would hammer on the wall, but it made no difference.

Mother wasn't the same after Rosina died. You'd never have known Rosina had lived, there was nothing of her left when we moved into number nineteen. Not that we had much to start with of course, no photographs or anything like that, but Rosina had a little spinning top. I often wondered where that little top went. Mother took to walking up and down the Butts; it was as if she couldn't bear to stay indoors. Father would often bring her home and put her to bed.

By the time I went out to work, Mother would spend most of her time sitting on her chair by the window in our room. She wouldn't speak. It was as if I wasn't there either, so I was happy to be going out and earning some money to help Father. Shall I tell you about that next?

Oh, the pot is empty. I say, those sandwiches look very nice. Will you excuse me while I visit the lav?

Interview 1 continued.

There, that's better out than in. Oh and look at these, cut into such dainty triangles and the crusts off! This is a real treat, I don't mind telling you. Are you sure you're getting all of this down? I don't know how you make all those marks on the page like that, it's not real writing is it? Shorthand, yes, I've heard of it. Never seen it before though, let me have a look now. Well, as long as you know what it says I suppose.

Where was I? Ahh yes, well Father sat me down when I was about 12, although I might have been still eleven, and told me it was time that I started paying my way. Bringing in some money. He was at the tin factory at the time and said he'd heard from one of his pals that there were places on the packing lines in the biscuit factory. You'll know all about Huntley and Palmer's, I'm sure.

[Huntley and Palmer was the main employer in Reading, and to some extent still is. Unmarried women have been employed for almost one hundred years to pack the biscuits.

The sister factory where the biscuit tins were made, Huntley, Bourne and Stevens, employs almost exclusively men. L.C.]

I was so excited to go with him the next day. I'd seen the girls all walking through town to get to the factory ever since I could remember and everyone knew they were good employers. You got to sit down, and even have a cup of tea in the afternoons. Father blacked my boots the night before and I had to wash my hands before we left. I remember Minnie shouting 'Good luck!' from the doorway of number four as we went past. She was working at Mrs Sparling's hat shop in Friar Street by then, in the backroom.

Father took me into the office area of the factory and told me to wait until my name was called. He had to get off to work so that he didn't lose a whole day's pay, so he left me sitting there. There were five other girls there, one I knew from school, Ada, she was a few months older than me, we smiled at each other. The other four I'd never seen before. They called Ada's name before mine and I was wondering how long she'd be when an older woman opened the door and called my name out. I hopped off the chair and followed her through the office and down into the factory. It was the biggest place I had ever seen. Rows and rows of girls and women at these long moving belts. Stacks of tins and lids and sheets of greased paper. Their hands moved so fast over the biscuits, grabbing the right number, wrapping them in the paper with a twist and then putting them into the tins. Oh, and I haven't mentioned the smell! In the packing room the smell was sweet, of the biscuits you understand. Out in the yards and when the wind was blowing the right way, it smelled more of the wet dough. You could tell what kind of biscuits they were making any day just by the smell. My favourites were Nice and Orange Drops, and Father liked the Ginger Nuts.

I was taken on to work in the packing room. I started at half past six in the morning and finished at six at night, Monday to Friday and we finished at midday on Saturdays. We could have our breakfast at about eight o'clock, and we'd stop for dinner at midday with a cup of tea at four. That was it though, no stopping at any other time else the biscuits would all drop into the broken bin at the end of the belt, and we'd be in trouble. No talking either, the managers were strict about that, but it was so noisy in there with the machines running the moving belts that you could hardly hear yourself think let alone what the girl next to you might have said.

The pay? Not enough, I know that much! Never is when it's young girls working. I think the most Father brought home was when he was taken on full-time and not just day labouring. He'd have brought home around fourteen or fifteen shillings a week then, unskilled as they called it. My first week's pay was eight shillings and thruppence, and a bag of broken biscuits. We all got a pound of brokens every week. But by the end of the second or third week, you'd be so sick of the smell, you wouldn't care if you never saw another biscuit again. Mother liked the brokens though. She'd lost most of her teeth by then, so she'd dunk them in her tea and then suck them.

I would give Mother six shillings a week and keep the rest. Father talked of moving us to bigger rooms, but we never did. I don't think Mother wanted to. People were always coming and going in the courts. It was like a little village right in the middle of town, everyone knowing each other, and each other's business. There were fights, men and women, and births and deaths as regular as clockwork. But going out to work meant I saw a bit more of life. Though in some ways working at the factory wasn't so different from being in the courts. The gossip was the same, always some girl giving another girl's chap the eye or more. Girls getting married; they'd have to leave the factory then, no married women were kept on. Girls going away to have babies, and sometimes coming back. One girl, Maud Stevens her name was, she got caught at least three times. Gave them all away, never said who the father was, or fathers it could have been I suppose. Just went away for a few days with her belly as round as a barrel and then back she came flat as a pancake. She was a bit simple though, was Maud. Had to have been to keep getting herself in that predicament over and over, and no man to claim the babies.

The factory was a good place though. They looked after us where some wouldn't have. But they had rules too. If you turned up with a dirty face or hands, you'd have your wages docked. Us girls had to go in and come out using a different entrance to the men. And another thing, we all had to pay in sixpence a week for the sick fund. Then if you died, your family would get a benefit, or if you got injured, you'd get a pension from the factory. There were a few old boys and girls who'd been at the factory for years, they were given light work until they couldn't work any longer. Iris was one of those. She would sit at the end of one of the moving belts and pick out any whole biscuits that might have been missed by the girls. The men would get a pension but not the women. I never understood why.

There were other entertainments too, if you paid a penny a week. You could use the library if you wanted to, though I never did. They put on lectures on Saturdays, I went to one or two of those, but I didn't really understand what they were about. There was an excursion, once a year in the summer. I went two or three times on those; we went to London on the train to the Crystal Palace, and to Henley by boat. We all wore our best frocks and hats and had a picnic lunch and ices. And they gave us all a day's paid holiday to go on the excursions too, I'd forgotten about that until just now with you asking. We had a very jolly time, Ada and me, before she left to get married. Oh, but the factory gave a wedding cake when you left to get married. Ada's was beautiful, one of her uncles worked in the icing room and he was allowed to decorate it. I remember it had tiny blue flowers like forget-me-nots around the edge.

Oh no, I never baked the biscuits, that was a man's job. I was on tin washing for a while. I didn't like that at all. We had these big baths full of hot water and suds and a scrubbing brush to get the baked-on biscuits off before the tins could be used again. There was no time to let them soak, you just had to scrub as hard as you could. When they made the Olivers, with the malt and black treacle, those were the worst tins to get clean. My hands got red raw from being in the water all day, they were cracked and bleeding after a while. No one stayed on tin washing for long, we all ended up the same way, and then we were sent back to the packing room or to label pasting. I did that for a while too, when my hands were getting better. At least we could sit down when we were label pasting. But you had to make sure they were straight and no creases. Then a boy would come and load the tins onto a trolley and take them off to the packing room.

They used small boys to pack the water tanks, you know. For the tins that were going abroad. The tanks only had a small hole in the top, but a boy could fit through it. Then a man would pass the boy each tin and the boy would pack them tightly inside. He'd stand on the last few, before he could climb out and put the last tin inside. Then the hole in the tank would be sealed. It meant the biscuits could be sent all around the world without getting spoiled. Some of the boys would talk about getting sealed inside, like stow-aways in a ship, and sailing around the world too. I don't think I would like that. Just going on the boat to Henley that one time was enough for me.

[I asked Mrs Hawkins about her time away from the factory at this point. I was keen to understand what role, if any, religion played in her life. L.C.]

Evenings in the week, I might go once or twice to a talk with Minnie or Ada. Only to the free ones, unless one of the girls had enough to pay for us all. Working in Friar Street, Minnie got to hear about everything that was going on. Sometimes we'd save for a couple of weeks and then go to a show. They had music nights at the Town Hall, so we'd go dancing, or there would be a proper show with singers and comedy acts, and we'd go and sing along with all the songs. Sometimes we'd get a bag of scraps on the way home. I enjoyed those shows a lot. I think they reminded me of Rosina and how she would spin around and dance.

We'd be paid on Fridays before we left the factory, and it was the same for Father when he was at the tin factory. He was there more often than on the railway when I was a bit older. Father would give Mother her housekeeping, but Father always paid the rent himself. I don't think he liked the landlord much. I don't think he wanted Mother to have to deal with him. Father would go to the pub on a Friday with his pals. Some of them lived in the courts, and some were from the tin factory. Father never came home drunk though. You write that down. Father could hold his drink. The times it would be him half carrying another fellow home to the courts, well I lost count.

I would stay home with Mother, but sometimes she wouldn't go to bed if Father wasn't home. Some nights she would just sit in her chair by the window, but others she would start to wail and call out for Father. Those nights I would go and fetch Father back home. I never liked going into the pubs to look for him. Everyone would turn and look when I opened the door, unless there was someone hanging around outside that I could ask to go in for me. I would ask at the bar if I couldn't see Father straight away. I looked older than I was, and some of the men were a bit too free with their hands, if you understand my meaning. I tried to get in and out as quickly as I could, but some Sundays I would see bruises where someone had grabbed me to take his chances.

There were three or four pubs where Father could be, and almost always he'd be in the last one I tried. I'd start at the Swan on the other side of the Butts, then the Sovereign in West Street, then the Cross Keys at the bottom of Broad Street, and if he wasn't in any of those, he'd be in the Boatman down towards the brewery. And if I decided to start looking at the Boatman, you could bet a week's wages Father would be in the Swan. Father didn't like me having to fetch him, his pals would make fun of him a bit, but he was the only one who could get Mother to bed on those nights. Even Mrs Draper couldn't get her to calm down, though she would sit with Mother while I went out.

On Saturdays after we finished work, if the weather was dry, Ada and I would sometimes walk along the canal and into the Forbury Gardens. In the summer there would be a brass band playing and we'd listen to them for a while. I think the bandstand is still there, you might go and have a look at it. If it was raining, or in the winter, we'd sometimes walk along Broad Street just looking in the shop windows and picking out all the nice things we'd buy when we got married. Or we'd have a cup of tea and an iced bun in Unwin's café. We never hurried home on a Saturday. It was the one day that everyone was out and about in the town centre.

Once Ada got engaged, we'd spend more time looking at things in the shop windows. And of course, Saturday afternoons were for weddings! We'd go and stand outside St Mary's or St Laurence's, or sometimes we'd walk all the way up to St Giles', just to see the brides in their dresses with their flowers. Ada would talk about the hats and flowers for ages afterwards.

It was about the only time I ever went near a church. Ada used to go on Sundays, her family went to St Laurence's by the Forbury. Father used to say that if Sundays were for rest, then he wasn't going to get up early just to be in a cold church. He would have me read from the Bible on Sunday afternoons though, so don't you go thinking we were heathens. Write that down. And of course, there was Rosina's funeral, though I don't remember going to that. I think I must have stayed with Mrs Draper. She's buried in St Mary's church yard, Rosina is, but you won't find a headstone for her.

Good Lord is that the time? I've got things to be getting on with, do you want that last sandwich? No? I'll just slip it in me handbag then, it'll do for the journey home. Same time next week, then. Cheerio!

Laura's first impressions

L aura had had an idea of the kind of woman Mrs Hawkins might be. She imagined the older lady to be coarse, stern, possibly foul-mouthed and with lose morals. As she watched the bulk of Mrs Hawkins hurry across the tea-room and out of the door into the sunshine, Laura frowned to herself. She looked down at her scrappy shorthand notes and hoped she would be able to read them again when she got home and had to type them up.

Mrs Hawkins had not matched the woman in Laura's imagination. She was older, yes, but had an air of pride and awareness about her that spoke of a sharp and appraising mind. She was well dressed and smartly turned out, her hair set and her nails clean and trimmed. Mrs Hawkins wore black, the costume of a widow; Lucy Worthington had mentioned she thought Mrs Hawkins had recently been bereaved.

Laura had taken Clive into her confidence in relation to the correspondence course and had sworn him to secrecy. Clive was smitten with Laura: he would have agreed to jump off Tower Bridge if she had asked it of him. He hoped she never would as he was not a confident swimmer. After paying the bill at the café, Laura made her way into the centre of London to do some shopping and to meet Clive for dinner. No longer needing to be chaperoned when in public, Laura and Clive had begun tentative discussions about their future together. He was making the right impression with the right people in the Foreign Office and was far more confident about his prospects there than in his swimming abilities.

If Clive could secure the job he wanted in the Diplomatic Service, he could marry Laura and they would embark on a life of adventure and endless receptions and dinners. It was what any girl would want in life, he was sure. His apartment in Belgravia would be retained for when they were in town, but Clive had his eye on a house in Oxfordshire where they could entertain and relax away from the city or when they returned from abroad. Clive was sure that once they were married, Laura would be content to manage both homes and would not pursue her current fascination with becoming a journalist.

He was waiting for her at the Savoy when Laura arrived at six o'clock. They dined early so that Laura could catch the train home again and be in bed before midnight. He noted with a smile the collection of bags and boxes that Laura handed to the service boy before she took off her coat.

Clive stood as Laura approached; she kissed his cheek while the waiter pulled out her chair. "You look radiant as ever," he said with genuine warmth.

"I look a fright. I got caught in a shower earlier and my hair has gone to frizz. I shall be glad to get home this evening."

"No drinks later, then. Understood. How did your meeting go with the mysterious Mrs Hawkins?"

The waiter appeared and it was not until their starters had been served that Laura replied to Clive's question.

"She is ... rather forthright. She told me a lot about her early years, far more than I was expecting in a first interview. I had hoped to have to ask some probing questions of her and tease out the information, but she chattered on happily for over an hour. She had a terrible start in life."

"In what way?"

"She grew up in the slum housing in Berkshire. Her older sister burned to death. Her mother seems to have gone mad with grief and her father was a labourer who couldn't earn or save his way out of the conditions his family found themselves in. It's all rather sad."

"Was she sad about it, this Mrs Hawkins?"

Laura considered the question as she pushed an asparagus spear around in its pool of Hollandaise sauce. "Not particularly, no. In fact, I got the impression that she was talking about someone else. I mean, when she was supposed to be talking about herself."

"Perhaps that's just how she has learned to cope with everything, to distance herself from it all as it were. I say, how many of these interviews do you think you'll have with her? If she's one of those women who need to be fed and watered, it's going to cost you a pretty penny."

"I'm not sure, perhaps three or four? I'm sure I can manage a few sandwiches and a pot of tea if it gets me the background for the article." She paused, the fork-speared asparagus dripping sauce onto her plate, "What do you mean, 'women who need to be fed and watered'? Is that how you see me?"

Clive looked up from his salmon mousse. "What? No, I just meant, well, women like that are often on the lookout for a ... well, a free lunch!"

Laura pondered Clive's assessment of Mrs Hawkins as she travelled out of the city later that evening. Was Mrs Hawkins in need of food?

She hadn't looked as if she were about to faint from starvation. There had been no discussion about Laura paying the woman for her time, but Laura now wondered if she should have offered. Money was such a delicate subject; if she offered, Mrs Hawkins might take offence and then where would Laura's article be? But if she didn't, was Mrs Hawkins suffering a hardship in giving up an hour of her time when she could be otherwise employed? Laura had no idea how to approach it. She felt insufficiently acquainted with Mrs Hawkins to risk losing her as a subject of inquiry.

Laura thought that Clive may have been correct in his analysis of Mrs Hawkins' apparent fake sadness at her sister's untimely death. Clive had suggested that witnessing such a tragedy would have had a lasting effect on a young child, who may have blocked out those memories and only in later years come to believe what they were told rather than what they had actually seen themselves. Could a five-year-old child really remember such graphic details as Mrs Hawkins had relayed to Laura? She thought it unlikely. That would explain the lack of real tears and emotion. The way Mrs Hawkins had explained the scene, was as if she were describing a film or a play. There was even a sense of enjoyment, Laura was certain, in being able to talk about such a horrendous event. Mrs Hawkins became the centre of attention rather than Rosina, Laura suddenly understood.

For a woman who had lived much of her life downtrodden and neglected, being listened to was perhaps all the payment Mrs Hawkins desired.

Interview 2.

[In our second interview, I wanted to encourage Mrs Hawkins to elaborate on her first marriage; I reminded her where we had finished previously and asked what she remembered about her friend Ada's wedding. I was also suffering with a head cold. L.C.]

What a filthy day it is out there! And the number thirty-seven bus is so unreliable these days, two came at once and both were crammed full. Still, here we are again. You keeping alright? Yes, you look a bit peaky. Better get some of that tea inside you, warm you up and bring a bit of colour back to your cheeks. Well no, as a matter of fact I haven't had anything since breakfast. Would you mind if I had a bowl of soup and a roll and butter? I believe I saw it was tomato soup today on the specials board. Thank you very much, I'm sure.

Ada was a beautiful bride, I can tell you that for nothing. Her family weren't well off you know. Her father was an insurance clerk down near the hospital, the Royal Berks, not Battle, and they only had a little house in Crown Street near the Red Cow. Ada and her mother made her wedding dress, and the veil came from her Granny Relph. Lovely bit of lace that was. And she had a flower girl and a page boy in very nice pale blue satin outfits, I believe they were her neighbour's children. Did I tell you about her wedding cake? Yes, I thought I did, tiny blue flowers on it like forget-me-nots and a blue ribbon around it. She had forget-me-nots in her bouquet, and white tulips all tied with another blue ribbon. They drooped a bit by the time it was all over, but they did look lovely when she arrived at St Laurence's.

Now, if you're wondering why Ada was married in St Laurence's when St Giles was closer and should have been her parish church, I know all about that. Ada's parents used to live in Leopold Road, and John's family were from Orts Road, so St Laurence's was their parish church from then. By rights, they should have got special permission to marry in St Laurence's but Ada never mentioned it so I would think their vicar just let them on account of them still being in the congregation.

I'd only been in that church once before. It was rather dark inside, I remember that much. But Ada was like an angel on her wedding day, she practically glided down the aisle to John's side. I never understood what she saw in him though. I suppose he was the first to take any notice of her, and the first to ask. His job? Didn't I say? He was a fishmonger. His father had a shop in Smelly Alley, that's Union Street to anyone who doesn't know Reading. John would take the deliveries out on his bicycle, and we'd often see him on Saturdays when we were on our way home from work. Ada's house must have been on his delivery round, now I come to think of it. He was a rather short fellow, but always polite, and never smelled of fish, which surprised me.

They had a wedding breakfast at the Red Cow after the service. Everyone got on the tram in Market Place and got off again the other side of the river at the end of London Street. Mrs Graham put on a lovely spread for them. She was the landlady there; her husband had run that pub for years before he died, and she had it herself for years afterwards. We all had a very jolly time of it, and then Ada and John went off to her parents' house so that she could get changed out of her frock before they caught the train to Newbury. John was opening his own fishmongers there, his father set him up as a wedding present, and Ada and John were to live in rooms over the shop.

[I asked Mrs Hawkins if she were sad that her friend was moving away. L.C.]

Sad? No, I wouldn't say I was sad. I was happy for them, to be living in Newbury. Nice place, not as busy as Reading you know, not as big. I missed going about with Ada if that's what you mean. She was a good friend, but by that time of course I'd already met Watmore.

This soup is very good. Are you going to leave your bread roll? Then you'll not mind if I have it, will you. You young girls these days, nothing of you and it's clear why. We always had to clear our plates you know. Father would have given us a right telling off if we'd left any food. Said he didn't work a fourteen-hour shift for us to be picky about what we ate.

Watmore? Yes, he worked. He was a bricklayer at the biscuit factory for a while, and then he worked on the new Simonds buildings when they extended the brewery. Now he was a handsome fellow. Tall and strong, always kept his moustache trimmed neat, big hands. He told a good tale as well, did Watmore. He would have the whole place hanging on his every word once he got started. He never came to Ada's wedding. I asked him if he would, but he was busy with something or other.

I met him when I was out looking for Father one evening. Watmore was in one of the pubs, I forget which one now but probably the Swan. He said I shouldn't be out on my own and he'd come with me to find Father as he knew him by sight. I must have been about sixteen then, it was a good year before Ada got married, I'm sure of that.

It wasn't courting as you might call it now. He didn't take me for walks around the Forbury or to a dance. That wasn't his way. He got to drinking with Father and sometimes they would come home together and Watmore and I would talk for a few minutes while Father put Mother to bed, before Watmore went home again. Sometimes he'd be outside the factory on a Saturday, and he'd walk with Ada and me into town. Or he'd knock on our door after Father had already gone out, and then he'd stay for a bit longer. Thomas was his Christian name, but everyone always called him Watmore, so I did too.

All the men drank. Unless they'd signed the pledge of course, and if they smelled beer on your breath at the biscuit factory, they sent you home without that day's pay. But they all still drank. Sometimes I'd have a gin now and again, but not often. I never really liked the taste, or how it made me feel, like my head was spinning. I like to keep my wits about me.

Watmore would get a bit loud when he drank. His favourite story to tell when he'd had a beer or two was of how he'd been before a judge for playing marbles in the street when he was just a little lad, he would say he was three years old. I don't know if it was true or not, but he told that tale ever so often, I think he must have believed it. He also got fined for being drunk and refusing to leave the premises when he was fourteen. It was his first wage and his workmates got him drinking, so he always said. His father tanned his hide for that and had to pay

Watmore's fine of forty shillings. I know that was true because Father said he'd heard the same from some of his pals about Watmore. So it must have been.

Watmore started coming to the courts more regular on a Friday after work. He must have been watching for Father to leave I think as there were only minutes between them some nights. Sometimes Father put Mother to bed before he went out. Well, one thing led to another, and eventually I had to tell Watmore that I thought I was pregnant.

He wasn't happy about it at first. He gave me a slap and told me I was stupid. No, it wasn't the first time, but he only did it when he'd been drinking whiskey and he was always so sorry afterwards. And I had been stupid. Stupid to think we could carry on like we had and I'd not fall at some point. I remember, Watmore stormed out and then came back about an hour later. I thought I might never see him again and that Father would have to have it out with him. It had been pouring with rain, just showers they were but real downpours that year. Watmore was soaked through when he came back. He told me we'd wait and see if I missed my next monthly. No point jumping the gun, he said.

Of course, I did. I knew I was carrying a baby, but I agreed with Watmore that we wouldn't say anything to anyone until we were sure. He did the right thing, mind you. He spoke to Father and said we wanted to get married. Father wasn't happy that it needed to be done quick, but he could hardly say no. Watmore had a job, and we were to stay with Mother and Father until the baby was born. We were married at the end of September 1890. Just Watmore and me, Father and Mother, Watmore's father Arthur, and the Drapers. Minnie was my bridesmaid. Ada couldn't come, she was ready to have her first baby around that time and John didn't want her to travel. They sent a lovely card though. Yes, we'd kept in touch by letter. I often think it was a good thing Father was so strict with us going to school. If I hadn't learned to write all those years ago, things would have been so much harder. Watmore wasn't so good at writing or reading. He was just good with his hands and he was always quick to work out the price of something. He knew the cost of everything and the value of nothing, Father would say.

The frock I wore for my marriage to Watmore was just a plain one, we had no money for fancy clothes. Minnie bought me a small posey of flowers, and of course we had the cake from the factory afterwards and a barrel of beer from the Plasterer's Arms. And that was it; I had to give up my job at the factory and do what I could to get ready for the baby. I'd saved a little bit, but that soon went once Watmore knew about it. No, he didn't steal it, it was our money together once we were married. He needed it, so he took it. He gave Father some housekeeping every week and we were saving for our own place too. A penny here and a penny there, it all adds up you know. For a while he wasn't even going out every Friday with Father.

As it happens, it was a Friday when Fred was born. That was a bad winter. I'd not known the cold to last for so long as it did that year. We were freezing from the end of November until the end of January and from Christmas it was so foggy it really got into your bones. People froze to death that winter. We kept Mother in bed as much as we could, wrapped up in blankets and coats. The streets were icy, you had to watch your step everywhere, and they say the Thames was frozen over but in London, not in Reading. I was hoping and praying that the baby would be late, hoping that the cold would break before he came.

It was the middle of the Thursday morning when it started. I had some idea of what was going on; you don't live that close to your neighbours and not pick up a thing or two over the years. No, I shan't put you off your soup with all the details, you must know how babies are born in any case. Young girls know everything these days. I made sure Mother was in bed, and then I went over to Mrs Draper. We'd agreed that I'd have the baby with her, she had the whole of the top floor of number four by that time and only Minnie and her two younger brothers still at home. Mr Draper was a drayman with Simonds. He was a funny little man, but kind too. All of the Drapers were kind people.

When Minnie came in from work, Mrs Draper sent her over to ours with some dinner for Mother. When Father and Watmore came home, Mrs Draper told them I'd be staying with her that night. She wouldn't let Watmore come in and see me. He started shouting until Father pulled him away. Watmore never cared much for Mrs Draper. Father called in again the next morning and Mrs Draper said everything was coming along nicely. I followed her down to the door so I could see Father, but Watmore had already gone to work. Mrs Draper spent that day between our two buildings, seeing to Mother and then coming back to me. Then Minnie sat with Mother that afternoon because I was so far along that Mrs Draper didn't want to leave me alone. Minnie had Friday afternoons off from work because the hat shop was open all day Saturday you see.

Fred was born at half past five in the afternoon. Frederick Thomas, we called him. Mrs Draper let Watmore come and see me and the boy for a few minutes once we were washed and settled, and then I didn't see Watmore again until the Thursday of the next week when I went back to our rooms. By all accounts he'd been drunk for much of that week and hadn't been to work at all until Father told him to sober up or get out.

[I asked what equipment they had for the baby and what it was like living in such cramped accommodation. L.C.]

I had an old fruit crate in the bedroom that was Fred's crib to start with. It had four small sheets cut from an old bedsheet and hemmed all round, and I'd knitted some little blankets for it. Snug as a bug, Fred was. Minnie had given me two tiny bonnets for him, and the rest of his clothes I'd either been given or I'd knitted from unravelling old sweaters. Of course, if we'd planned any of it, I'd have had Fred in the summer when he could have been outside and not needing anything to soak up his waste. I had some felt squares from an old horse blanket that I used for that.

It was harder work than I'd ever imagined it would be. Getting clothes and bedding dry was the hardest thing, it was still so cold and we only had that tiny fireplace. My hands were red and cracked from all the scrubbing and then Fred got a bad rash and we had to get some ointment for him. Watmore wasn't happy about that on account of how much the doctor cost. He said I shouldn't have listened to Mrs Draper, and that I should have just gone to Timothy Whites on Broad Street and got their chemist to make something up for it.

It was a little while after that when Watmore came home and said he'd heard of a place that wanted an extension built and was looking for builders. It was in Bermondsey. Yes, I know, that's your neck of the woods isn't it. Funny how these things go. Anyway, Watmore said he could earn enough money doing that job for a few weeks to mean we could move out of West Court into our own place.

He'd been gone a week when he wrote to Father to say there was a job for me at the house if I could find someone to look after Fred. Watmore had fallen in with the Head Groom there and had told them I was his sister. I didn't want to leave Fred, but I missed Watmore already and missed working at the factory with the other girls. I thought if I could do it just while Watmore was there then we'd be better off. Father wasn't in agreement; he didn't hold with lying and thought

Watmore should be able to support us without expecting me to work as well. He'd grown fond of Fred too, just in that short time. It was Mrs Draper who helped us again with it all. She said she would look after Fred, and Mother during the day, until Watmore and I came back. Of course, that upset Watmore when I told him how we'd arranged everything, but he went along with it in the end.

The place that was having the extra portion added on was a big old house with so many windows. It reminded me of the Palmer's house in Prospect Park. It belonged to a Surgeon and his family; they had six children and his wife adored cats. There were cats everywhere, all different colours and sizes. They were allowed to go wherever they pleased in the house, but never outside, and I was forever having to clean up after them. The Surgeon's butler took me on as an under-maid, which meant I was the lowest servant in the house and had to keep out of everyone's way. If the Surgeon or his wife came into a room I was in, I had to leave immediately no matter what I was doing. I tell you, if I thought my hands were sore from washing Fred's things, they were ten times worse by the time I left Bermondsey. I hated it there. I shared a tiny room with the other under-maid, Kitty, who was only fifteen. I thought I'd be able to see Watmore but we hardly were together for five minutes the whole time. He said we had to be careful because everyone there thought we were brother and sister. Of course, I missed Fred too, but I was so tired at the end of every day I barely thought of anything or anyone except work after the first week or so.

We were in Bermondsey for just over six months. When we came back to Reading, Fred was so big! And Minnie was pregnant but wouldn't say who the father was. I think she was more sad that I'd come back to take Fred than her mother was. Watmore said he'd give Mrs Draper some money for taking care of Fred, but I found out later that he never did. He gave Minnie all the clothes Fred had grown out of though. Watmore hadn't been drinking hardly at all while we were in Bermondsey, but he made up for it when we got back.

We moved out of West Court and over to Bedford Court in Chatham Street. On the corner of the court was the White Lion pub. I used to wonder if that's why Watmore moved us over there, so close to a pub. But then, Reading had so many more pubs in those days, Simonds wasn't the only brewery in the town, but it was the biggest. A lot of places were owned just by the landlord and not by a brewery. The Irish lived mostly around Chatham Street. It was close to the horse market. No, Watmore wasn't Irish, but he liked to go about with them.

Bedford Court was not so different to West Court; still tall buildings built around a square of cobbles, but the square was a little larger I should say. We had the top floor of building two, which was three rooms, and a privy and a water pump in the back yard just for our building. For a while, we were the only family there who weren't Irish. I didn't get along with the other women, and truth be told, I couldn't understand what they were saying half the time. They had their own language you see; it wasn't just their accents. I don't think they liked me much either, but they all liked Watmore. Everyone did. It was noisier than West Court on account of being much closer to the railway. Market days would be noisy too, all the cows and horses as well as the auctioneers and all their nonsense. Have you heard them? How anyone understands what they say I shall never know. Watmore liked to go to the auctions with his pals, and then they would stop off at the White Lion before coming home. I don't know why he liked the auctions; he didn't know anything about the animals. But he would say he was making connections, whatever that meant.

I would walk back over to West Court most days when I had swept and cleaned our rooms. Mrs Draper was happy to see me, and Minnie liked to coo over Fred as her time got closer. She still wouldn't say who the father was. She planned to leave her baby with Mrs Draper and go off to London to work as a milliner. She did too. She met a young man there and got married after they set up their own little shop. Took her daughter back, which broke Mrs Draper's heart, but then they had Mrs Draper move in with them when Mr Draper passed away.

Watmore didn't have a steady job when we came back from Bermondsey. He'd get day labour sometimes with his Irish pals, and sometimes he'd be taken on for building jobs. He never worked at the factory again. I remember just after we'd moved to Bedford Court, Watmore was arrested. He had gone to watch a fire in Friar Street, one of the warehouse buildings at the corner where it met Chatham Street was burning and there was quite a crowd gathered there by all accounts. The police constables were trying to move the crowd on so that the firemen could get their wagon closer to the blaze. Of course, the crowd didn't want to be moved, it was quite a spectacle and certainly entertaining for those looking on. A scuffle broke out and Watmore was bashed on his head by a police constable's truncheon! They arrested him and he was up before a judge the next day. It wasn't unusual for Watmore not to be home at nights, and the first I heard of it all was when he came home the following day. The judge had thrown out the charges against Watmore and the other fellow he was with. But Watmore was raging about it, saying how he knew where the constable lived, and he'd see more flames before the week was out.

Watmore was never the same after that bash to his head. He would spend more time out with his pals and less time working. Those were hard days, mark my words. There were times when I went without so that the children could have something to eat. Well of course, more children came along regular as clockwork. I don't have to explain to you how that happens, do I? I'd rather not, if it's all the same to you.

When Fred was two, I had Alice. I wanted to call her Rosina after my sister, but Watmore insisted she be named after his mother. Then two years later I had another girl, so she was called Rosina. I had argued with Watmore over her name, and I should have known better because she only lived a few hours.

I fell pregnant with George almost straight after having Rosina. There was almost exactly a year between them. All my children with Watmore were born early in the year; Watmore always said how much he liked April and May time with the blossoms on the trees and the days getting longer and warmer. He was always in good spirits then. I remember the Queen's jubilee, her diamond one in '97, was one of the nicest times we had as a family together. We took the children down to the river to watch the boat races, and then we went back in the evening for the fireworks. Fred loved the boats. There was a long procession through the town from Market Place in a circle along Friar Street, then down West Street and back along Broad Street. They stopped the trams and there were such crowds of people all in their best clothes. Flags were hung up on every building, and all of the shop windows had displays in red, white and blue. The factory made special jubilee biscuits and Simonds sold jubilee pale ale. Yes, that was a lovely day out for us.

Ernest came after George, and I must have fallen for him over that jubilee week. He came too early though and was a quiet baby, not like the others. I'd been down in the yard doing the washing. Watmore said he'd just stopped breathing. When the next baby came a year later, Watmore said we should call him Ernest as well, seeing as the other one hadn't grown into his name before he died. I didn't argue; Watmore named all of our boys.

So there were six of us at Bedford Court, we lived there for about ten years. The last year we were there was the worst. Watmore would have such terrible headaches, he would weep with the pain when he thought no one was looking. He spent more and more time with his Irish pals, and though he brought money home, I can't say that it was all from working, if you know what I mean. It kept us out of the workhouse though.

Some of the Irish families had moved out of the court by then and more people were coming in from the countryside to find work. There were other families too, some Jews, some other foreigners. Gawd, if I thought the wet dough smell from the factory was bad, the smell from some of the neighbours cooking would make your eyes water! I've no idea what was in it, but I've smelled the same sometimes when I've been along Warwick Way in Pimlico, and along Dalson Lane in Hackney. Gets in the back of your throat. I'm not sure I could eat whatever it is.

I still went over to visit Mother and Mrs Draper once or twice a week. I would see Fred and Alice off to school on the Oxford Road and then take George and Ernest with me. I got home one day to find Watmore on the floor of our bedroom, in just his shirt and socks, dead. I was thankful I only had the two youngest with me, I took them straight over to old Mrs Woodley on the other side of Chatham Street and then went on to fetch a doctor. I knew Watmore couldn't be saved, but the doctor would be the one to make everything official and above board. They said it was Watmore's brain, it had been bleeding inside his skull. I often wondered if it was from that blow with the truncheon, but we never knew for sure.

They took him down to the Battle hospital and said we could make our own arrangements or if we couldn't afford a burial that the Corporation would take care of it, and I'd have to pay them back in instalments. Well, we all know what that means!

[I said I did not and could Mrs Hawkins explain. L.C.]

Anyone dies in the poor house and has no family to claim them, their remains go to the hospital. For the doctors to do their training on. Cutting people up like that, I don't know how they stomach it, I'm sure. We were lucky with Rosina and Ernest, Watmore had money to cover their burials, though we had no wake or anything like that. But when Watmore died I didn't think we had any money beyond the few pennies I had in a tin on the bedroom mantlepiece. I don't know why, but when the doctor had gone to fetch the ambulance, I went through Watmore's pockets. I didn't expect to find much, maybe a book of matches or a piece of string, a few pennies, you know the sort of thing men keep on their person.

You can imagine my surprise when my fingers felt paper. You'll remember I said Watmore was no good at reading or writing? Even that letter he'd sent Father saying I should go to Bermondsey was written by the groom. But what I pulled out of his trouser pocket along with a handful of shillings and tanners was a bundle of scraps of paper with names and numbers on, and three folded five-pound notes! I'd never seen real paper money before, we always got paid in shillings at the factory, and it took me a moment to understand what it was.

There was a knock at the door, and I stuffed the notes and coins into my apron pocket. That was a strange day, I can tell you. One after another, Watmore's pals came to our door to pay their respects and all of them offering to see us right for the funeral and wake. I didn't know what to say, my mind was all of a whirl. Some brought their whole families with them. We'd never had so many people in our rooms as that day, not even when the babies had passed on.

As I said, everyone liked Watmore.

Shall we have a pot of tea?

Interview 2 continued.

I f Watmore hadn't died, I might never have met Harry. They were pals, though not close. Harry knew Watmore from when they were laying bricks together at Simonds. He came round a couple of days after Watmore's funeral, when the fuss had died down. Said he'd read about it in the newspaper and wanted to make sure we were provided for. Well, we had enough to be getting on with; Watmore's Irish friends had explained to me what the scraps of paper were and said they would sort everything out and call in the debts owed to him. It turns out he'd been running books at dog fights. I told Harry I was thinking of leaving the Court and taking a small house somewhere. I thought I might take in a lodger to keep our heads above water. I was getting on, thirty that year, had four children to think of, and I'd even considered asking Father if he and Mother would come in with me.

Harry said not to make any rash decisions. He was a kind man, was Harry Jones. Nothing at all like Watmore, not tall and strong, not loud and certainly not a drinker. Harry was as tall as me, and really didn't look like he could lay bricks all day. He was a good few years younger than Watmore too, younger than me if you must know, by three years. He was living in a boarding house along the Oxford Road, and he would call in on his way home from work most days for his dinner.

It still took me by surprise when he proposed marriage. I'd have been happy to carry on as we had been, and the children were settled again at school after a bit of trouble with George there when Watmore died. Harry came in one day at the beginning of February with a bunch of daffs, it was my birthday, and I was thanking him for them and telling Alice to find a jug to put them in when I turned around and Harry was down on one knee! He said he had no ring, and hadn't been to see Father, but would I consider making things permanent between us. His face was so serious, you'd think he was signing his life away, and I suppose he was in taking on a widow with four children. I told him to get up off the floor and stop embarrassing himself.

I didn't mean to be horrid to him, but I was getting dinner ready, and I'd only end up tripping over him kneeling there. He was silent during the meal; I remember it very clearly. When we'd finished, I sent Alice to wash the plates and the boys to their room. I sat Harry down and we talked it all through. I wanted to be sure he understood what he was asking me. He was such a dear man, and I felt he could do better than us. In truth, I didn't think I was worth his attention. I would have settled for another like Watmore at the drop of a hat, but Harry was a good, kind man, and I felt for him more like a brother than a lover. He wouldn't give it up though. He said I should think about it, and he'd ask again a week later.

I kept that poor man waiting another year and a half before I agreed, and only then because I was about to have Emily and I'd made him ask Father. We were married in April 1903, at St Mary's. It was another small ceremony; I didn't want any fuss with me being a widow and six months pregnant. Harry was working for the Queen's Road Dairy by then as a milkman and had started taking Fred out with him some mornings on the cart. We moved to a house on Rupert Street in Newtown and the children went to the school next to the laundry. I liked that little house. It had so much more room and a small yard at the back where I could do our washing. They were called slums though, those houses. I don't know why, they were a hundred times better than the courts.

George didn't settle at Newtown school. He was nine and never took to Harry like the rest of them did. I never understood it, Fred got along famously with Harry and loved going out on the milk cart with him. Ernest was a happy chap and got along with everyone just like his father. But George was a sulky child. If something broke, it would be George that broke it. If something went missing, George would have it. And the arguments, cor lummy that boy would answer back as quick as you like! He would play out with the Cornell twins, Eric and Patrick, and the scrapes they would get into, as well as the fights between them all, and then they would be best friends again the next day. They would skip school and hang around the gas works and the back of the biscuit factory.

Harry tried to deal with him, but he was too soft. I took a stick to George several times, but it did no good. Then one day the truant inspector came to our door wanting to know where George was. I told him, he's at school where he should be. He wasn't though, George and the twins had gone all the way to Palmer Park and had been throwing stones at the windows in the gymnasium! Of course, Mr Cornell blamed George for leading his boys astray, though everyone knew they were as bad as each other. We tried punishing George, we tried bribing him, but nothing would get that boy to stay in school. Harry even sat him down and explained that if he didn't stay in his classes, Harry and me could end up going to prison. I could see by the look on George's face the thought of Harry in prison was not having the effect that Harry had hoped it might.

It got so that the truant inspector was at our door almost every week. Harry was at his wits end. In November 1904 we got a letter telling us we had to go to the school for a meeting with the people from the Education Board. On the days that George did stay more than an hour or so, he ended up fighting with the other boys and the school had had enough of him as well. Harry arranged for Fred to take Dolly and the milk cart out that morning and we met with the Board and constable Oldham was there too, I remember his big bushy eyebrows. They said they felt it would be in George's interests to go away to a technical school. We had to sign some papers and then they took him straight away. I wanted him to have his clothes, but they said he wouldn't need them, and he'd have a uniform when he got to the new school.

Harry said he felt like a failure. He took it all to heart, even though I told him George was just like his father and there wasn't anything more we could have done about it. Harry got a bee in his bonnet about the neighbours gossiping about us and about George. I told him to ignore them, and no one said anything of it to my face even if they were saying it behind my back – and I knew they were. Even though the truant inspector called at everyone's house down Rupert Street at least once a year, it was always George that those women gossiped about, and it was always my fault. I was either too soft or too hard on the boy. I walked into the butcher's once and Mrs Delaney was in full flow about how women like me should have all our children sent away. I told her, at least all my children knew their fathers. That shut her up.

It wore Harry down though. In the end he got a job with the Caversham Dairy and we moved over there for a while. I was very sorry to leave Rupert Street. I wrote to George with our new address, but he was never one for writing.

Excuse me while I nip to the lav.

[I tried to compose myself while Mrs Hawkins was away from our table. Her matter-of-fact retelling of her son being removed from the home seemed cold and callous and had shocked me. When she returned, I attempted to find some compassion underneath her hard exterior. L.C.]

You seem a bit preoccupied with people feeling sad, if you don't mind me saying, Miss Curtly. We didn't have time to mope around being sad. You just got on with things. I told you, we'd done all we could to get George to behave himself, what else were we supposed to do? I had four other children to consider. We had to make the best of it, and George would be looked after, and better things would come of it for him. That's what we were told, and we had to trust the authorities.

Alice didn't come with us to Caversham. She was ready to leave school and got a job at the laundry. Now, you ask me about being sad: I was sad that Alice decided to stay with our neighbour in Rupert Street and not come with us. She was such a help to me with the others, and especially when I had Emily. Fred came but he had to get the tram back across the river every day because he'd got a job in the biscuit factory. They had him doing general labouring work, whatever needed doing. He always said he wouldn't be there forever, he wanted to take advantage of the instructional talks they had for the workers. Fred always had his nose in a book or the newspaper. He's in London now, got himself some kind of politics job after the war. Doing very nicely by all accounts but not married. No, I don't hear from him very often.

We had a bit of trouble in Caversham. Not with the children this time, but with our landlord. Harry was so determined to move away from Rupert Street that he came home one day and said he'd found us rooms to rent in a house and we were moving in that weekend. I had two days to sort everything out, pack what I could into boxes and make sure Alice had her keep paid up for the following week with our neighbour. Two days! We used the milk cart, which is why we had to go on the Saturday afternoon because it was Harry's last day at the dairy and the cart and Dolly had to go back.

We got to the address, it was next door to the hotel just over Caversham bridge on Bridge Street, and there was no one at home to let us in. Harry was banging on the door when a window opened above our heads. A woman called down to us to ask in the hotel for the landlord. Harry went into the hotel and found the landlord, who had completely forgotten the conversation he'd had with Harry and had let the rooms to someone else in the meantime! There we were, in the street with all our belongings on show, homeless. Emily was cutting her teeth and was grizzling, Fred was upset because he'd turned down going to see a football match with his work pals to help us get moved in, and only Ernest seemed untroubled by it all. He just sat on the back of the milk cart sucking on a barley sugar that Harry had bought him as a treat.

We couldn't go back to Rupert Street, not just because a new family had arrived half an hour before we left that morning ready to move in with all of their furniture, but the embarrassment of being let down would have set the gossips off again. Harry wouldn't entertain the idea. Instead, he talked to the hotel owner for some time and managed to arrange for us to use two rooms for a week so that we could at least unload the cart and get it back to the dairy. We would have our meals in the hotel and our laundry done, but only for the one week and Harry would have to find us somewhere else to live. I did take pity on him, I'm not such a hard woman to kick a man when he's already down, and it wasn't really Harry's fault that the landlord had forgotten. He was harder on himself than ever I could be.

Luckily, Harry did have his new job at Caversham dairy to go to. That meant on the Monday morning he could have a good look at the streets on his round and ask about any houses that looked empty. Fred was at work, and I decided not to send Ernest to school just in case we had to move on again and away from the area at the end of the week. I suppose he would have taken it all in his stride as he did with everything else, but he was easy to have around. The weather was fine, and while Harry slept in the afternoons, I took the children for walks along the river, up around the Warren to see the big houses there, and up Saint Peter's Hill towards Emmer Green. And it was on one of my walks that I saw the house we eventually moved into.

Harry had seen it too and had been trying to find out who owned it through the men at the dairy. I knocked at the house next door and met a pair of elderly sisters who invited us in for tea. They were lovely ladies, Miss Georgina and Miss Sarah Higgins. Both long gone now I'm afraid, but I couldn't have asked for better neighbours. It turned out that they owned the house next door, as well as the one they were living in and another across the street that had a tenant. Their father had invested in the houses and left them to the sisters on his death. When I explained our situation they took pity on us, particularly when I said that Harry had a good job with the dairy and that Fred was also at work. Emily was thankfully sleeping in my arms, but I think it was Ernest who charmed them the most. He sat quietly with his big eyes watching them and swinging his legs under his chair until a dog started barking somewhere in the house.

The sisters looked at the clock in the corner of their drawing room and said it must be time for Jack's biscuit. Miss Sarah went out of the room and came back moments later with a small white terrier in her arms. She put him down in front of Miss Georgina, and the little dog lifted one front paw and then the other as if to shake hands. That set Ernest off giggling. The dog's little tail was wagging away, and Miss Sarah broke a biscuit in half, giving one piece to the dog and the other to Ernest. I thought for a moment he would eat it himself, he was always putting things in his mouth, but Miss Sarah held on to it in his hand, and called the dog over. Jack sat down again in front of Ernest and lifted his paws as before, and then Ernest gave him the biscuit. Well, those two were firm friends from that moment onwards!

I didn't want to outstay our welcome, but the sisters said they would speak with their solicitor the next morning and if Harry and I would call on them the following afternoon they would show us inside the house. Harry was not as happy about it as I thought he might be. He had wanted to sort out our mess himself, but he came back to the hotel the next day, had a wash and some lunch, and then we all went back to Albert Road.

We couldn't afford it of course. A three-bedroom villa with two rooms downstairs plus a big kitchen, running water, and an indoor lav. It was a palace compared to Rupert Street, but we couldn't stay in the hotel, and we had enough money to cover the first few weeks' rent. I'd been able to save most of what Watmore had left me once the debts had been called in and we'd managed on Harry's wages up to then. So we signed the sisters' papers and we moved our things across the following weekend.

I really think you should get yourself off home to bed, you don't look at all well. Go on now, and we'll carry on next week.

Laura is confined to bed

C live was not a regular visitor to the schoolhouse. He preferred to stay in the Knightsbridge and City areas where he could see and be seen, and occasionally pick up a snippet of political gossip or intrigue. However, when Laura was taken ill, he made an exception to bring her some flowers. Mrs Curtly kept him in the sitting room for as long as she could, plying him with tea and cakes, but in the end, she accepted that Clive was there to see her daughter and reluctantly directed him up the stairs.

Laura would naturally have liked some warning of her suitor's visit. Her hand-mirror was out of reach, but she knew she must look a fright after a week in bed with the influenza. She imagined her face would be pale and skeletal, her hair lank and dishevelled. She wriggled herself up to a sitting position and pulled her bed-jacket closer around her shoulders as Clive nudged her bedroom door open cautiously.

"How are you, old girl?"

"Dreadful. And now the indignity of being seen in such a state on top of it all."

"I can go if ..."

"No! No, come in. Pull up the stool there. The window is open and I'm sure I am no longer contagious."

"I say, you don't think you caught it from your Mrs Hawkins do you?"

"Don't be absurd, Clive. I was feeling out of sorts before I saw her last week. Really, she's not some plague-ridden hag you know." Laura coughed into her handkerchief and waved her hand towards a glass of water on her dressing table which Clive retrieved for her.

"I still wonder if you're doing ... Oh, Mrs Curtly, here let me take those!" Clive jumped up as Laura's mother brought the vase of flowers into the room.

"No need, I'm sure. There, Laura, aren't they beautiful? Mr Merton is such a thoughtful young man. Shall I bring you more tea?"

"No thank you, Mother. I shall survive a few more minutes on water."

"Well, I'll leave the door open. Do come down if you would like anything at all, Mr Merton."

When her footsteps had receded out of earshot, Clive took up his previous train of thought.

"I was about to say, I wonder if you're doing the right thing by getting involved with a woman like that. Can you really be sure she's not harbouring some communicable disease?"

"She's not some Dickensian character! In fact, she looked the very picture of health the last time I saw her. Robust is a descriptor that springs to mind. Robust and resilient."

"Really? What tale did she tell you this time?"

"We talked about her job at the biscuit factory, about her friend getting married and then how she and her husband went to work in Bermondsey leaving their baby boy behind. They made enough money to move to their own home, and she had a further four ... no, wait, let me see, there was Fred, Alice, Rosina, she died, George and Ernest, oh but the first Ernest also died so Ernest number two. No, I was wrong, she had five more children with this Watmore fellow before he died."

"They do breed so, the lower classes."

"Clive!"

"I'm sorry old thing, but it's the truth. One only has to look out of the omnibus window and see the hoards of children in rags around London. It is truly irresponsible when the parents don't have two farthings to rub together."

"Well, that's where the story takes a twist. Mrs Hawkins did come into some money when Watmore died. Not a lot, I grant you, but it must have seemed like a fortune to her at the time. And she found love too."

Clive laughed, and then stopped when he realised Laura was not sharing his merriment.

"Her second husband sounds a jolly decent chap. He was a brick-layer who then worked as a milkman."

"At least he was employed I suppose. You seem rather more fond of Mrs Hawkins than after your first meeting. She's growing on you isn't she. Be careful though darling, you still really know nothing about her."

"I know that two of her children died when they were very young, just a few days old. That must have been terribly upsetting for her, but do you know, just like when she told me her sister had died, there was no real emotion from her. She didn't even pretend to be upset this time."

"Sounds like she has perfected the stiff upper lip if you ask me. And it must have been some years ago. Time moves on."

"But to lose a child. To lose two. I don't think I could bear it. I'd rather not have any children at all than to see them die at any age let alone so young."

Clive reached forward and patted Laura's hand gently. "There, there, don't upset yourself over it. These things happen."

"And then the trouble she had with George. Did you ever play truant from school?"

"Truant? Good Lord, no. Not really possible when one is a boarder."

"I hadn't thought of that. They sent him away."

"Who did, Mrs Hawkins?"

"No, the Education Board. They sent George to London to a trade school or something of the sort."

"I suppose it was for the best."

"That's what Mrs Hawkins said to me. One less mouth to feed I suppose. She does seem genuinely to have feelings for her second husband though. His name was Jones, Harry Jones. Curiously, she said she didn't want to marry him at first but that she would have taken up with another like Watmore just like that!"

"Well, women like that often have a type."

"What do you mean?"

"Some women seem to prefer the hardship. If they are mistreated, they stay with the chap. If they do manage to get away, invariably they then take up with another cut from the same cloth. They don't look outside of their own class, their own kind, for a husband. It's a jolly good thing too, because they'd have rum luck trying to find a husband from the better classes."

Laura closed her eyes and sank back into her pillows. Was Clive right in his summing up of the female behaviour in the lower classes? She supposed he must be, as so few women appeared able to marry above their station. And as Mrs Hawkins had said, once married, the children appeared as regular as clockwork. Laura wished she could do something to help those who found themselves in distress.

"Laura? Shall I go, if you need to sleep?"

"I'm sorry, I was just going over again what Mrs Hawkins had said. Some of the things, well they sound so fantastic that I wonder if they can really be true. But then, she has no reason to make them up, does she?"

"Like what?"

"Oh I don't know … well, can one really make much money from betting on dog fights?"

Clive's eyebrows shot up in surprise. "Are we still talking about Mrs Hawkins?"

"No, her husband, the first one, Watmore. She said when he died, she found some, I suppose they must be what people call betting slips, and fifteen pounds in his pockets."

"Good heavens! I've never been to a dog fight of course, but if it's anything like horseracing then I would think it possible to make rather a lot of money, yes. But dog fighting, honestly Laura, I don't think you should continue with these interviews if that's the kind of woman she is."

"I told you, it was Watmore and not Mrs Hawkins. And it was a long time ago." Laura started to cough again, and after another sip of water she told Clive she was tired after all and perhaps he should let her sleep. He obeyed, his brow creased with worry over the way Laura seemed to be becoming attached to Mrs Hawkins. The sooner he could marry Laura the better it would be for everyone, he thought.

Laura listened to Clive's footsteps descend the stairs. She was very fond of him and didn't want to upset him. She also didn't want to fail the last assignment of her course. She was enjoying the process of taking dictation and then typing up her interviews afterwards on the new typewriter her parents had bought for her birthday along with a reem of paper. Laura was also enjoying hearing about Mrs Hawkins' life and living vicariously through the escapades with the older woman. If the tale had such an effect on Laura, surely it would be gripping for a newspaper or magazine audience as well.

There might even be a happy ending, Laura mused as she settled back down under the covers to doze. If nothing else, Mrs Hawkins had survived to tell her tale. If only Laura could shake off the 'flu before their next appointment.

Interview 3.

You look much better today, Miss Curtly, much better indeed. Thank you for getting the message to me, I stayed and had a cup of tea and then went to visit a friend, so my journey here wasn't a waste.

Remind me where we'd got to again. Oh yes, Caversham, that's it. Well, I should say those were the happiest days of my life. We had that lovely house, and Kitty was born there in 1907. Alice would come for her lunch on Sundays and Harry and Fred dug over the garden and we had vegetables to eat even when we didn't have any meat. There was an apple tree at the end of the garden and some old blackcurrant bushes, so the children had some fruit. And the rhubarb, oh my goodness we had some enormous sticks from that plant. It must have been all the muck from Harry's horse. He had two while we were in Caversham; Petunia and Florrie. I made sure to share what we grew with the sisters next door to keep in their good books, because sometimes we were a little bit late with the rent and the children could be noisy.

Ernest loved that dog, Jack. It broke his heart when we had to leave, and he begged me to let him have a dog of his own, but we couldn't. Things changed for us in the winter after Kitty was born. Fred had been ill for a few days with the influenza, and then Harry came down with it. Nothing as bad as the Spanish one, that was a few years later. No, this was just a nasty winter malady and we all had it eventually, and the sisters next door too. Harry had it and it went straight to his chest. He couldn't work, and every time he thought he could shake it off, he went downhill again even worse than before. Of course, while he wasn't working, we had no money coming in apart from Fred's housekeeping for the rent. Ernest was still at school, and I had the girls to look after. I had to swallow a bit of my pride and asked around, took in a bit of mending, but it wasn't enough.

Harry, as you might have realised by now, was a worrier. He didn't want us to get so far into debt that we'd be taken to court or the workhouse. We discussed it, and we agreed that he would see if he could get his old job back with the dairy in town, and that we'd move back into Reading to somewhere smaller. None of us wanted to go, we'd all grown to care for the sisters next door and Ernest was doing well in school. I suppose we'd begun to get ideas above our station living in Albert Road. It was such a lovely street, with the ladies saying, 'Good morning,' and 'Good afternoon,' when you passed them and the men mostly working in Reading with their suits and hats. I know it was a million miles away from what I grew up with, but I wanted the children to have the better air and a bit of space to run around without getting into trouble. I took some convincing, but Harry was a sensible man. He made me see sense in the end.

Harry had no trouble getting his job back. Caversham Dairy were sorry to see him go, as he'd been reliable until his illness. They had no sickness scheme there though, and no pension to pay into, not like the biscuit factory. But he was weak, he never really was well again after that illness. It was like he was having trouble breathing right, sometimes even when he was sitting down. He'd aged too. Now, I was no spring chicken, but Harry looked like he was older than Watmore by the time he went back to the town dairy. His hair had thinned and gone white in patches, and his skin was very pale, you could see his veins on the back of his hands. The town dairy gave him his old horse Dolly back though and he was happy about that.

We moved back to Reading, all our things on the milk cart again, at the end of September 1909. I was pregnant with Lily, but Alice came to help us settle in and Fred was still with us. It rained like the heavens were a river that day. Everything was soaked through before we even crossed Caversham Bridge. All of us were thoroughly miserable, the children were squabbling, Fred and Harry were worn out from loading the cart and my feet were swelling up like balloons. The sisters had given me a basket of jams and pickles as a farewell gift. We had that for our tea later that day with some crackers that Fred had brought home.

Harry had got us two rooms at the bottom of Southampton Street. Keep in mind how we'd been at West Court, all living on top of each other, and Bedford Court was no better, you'd think we'd have settled down easily in Southampton Street by St Giles church. We'd got a taste for the better life though, being over in Caversham in a nice house with good food. Our rooms in Southampton Street were at the back of a tall building with a tannery across a small yard from us. It stank to high heaven! There's no nice way of saying it. The ammonia stung your eyes from the moment you woke up until you went to sleep again and everyone in that building was coughing their guts up morning noon and night.

You can imagine how it affected Harry! We'd been there two or three weeks when he had his accident. He was in the dairy yard on his own, loading his cart. Dolly needed a new shoe, so Harry was working Bluebell that day. She was the sweetest horse you'd ever meet, so I know for a fact that she didn't knock Harry down on purpose. I've no idea how he came to be between Bluebell and the cart, but somehow he fell and she pulled the cart over him. It wouldn't have been so bad, but it was at the start of his round, so the cart had a full load of milk on it. They took him off to Battle hospital; we couldn't afford the doctors at the Royal.

[Mrs Hawkins became somewhat reticent at this point. It was two or three minutes before she spoke again in answer to my question as to whether Harry had survived his accident. L.C.]

Well now, no, he didn't, but it took him a while to pass on. And what was I to do in the meantime, I ask you? I had Alice wanting to come home to us again, she'd had a falling out with our old neighbours over something or other, George was meant to be leaving the Technical School at Christmas, and I had Lily on the way like I said. If Fred hadn't still been at the biscuit factory, I don't know what we'd have done.

The Corporation had built what they called apartments about half-way up Silver Street, that's the next road over to Southampton Street. They'd been there about ten years, but still looked neat and tidy with a garden in the middle where you could hang out your washing, and space at the back to put your ashes and other rubbish and the Corporation would take it all away. Jubilee Square it was called, though most people just called them the Silver Street flats. I was out with the girls doing a bit of shopping one day and I took a fancy to have a look at those apartments. I knew they were small, but you couldn't smell the tannery from Silver Street, so I asked one of the tenants what the rent was and how a person might be offered one.

Remember, Harry was in the workhouse. Yes, they moved him from the infirmary ward at the hospital into the workhouse even though he couldn't work. He told me he'd do it, so that he wouldn't be a burden on us all. Such a kind man was Harry. I say he couldn't work; he could hardly get out of bed. For a while they thought he had tuberculosis but it was just his lungs being damaged by the influenza and then being run over by his cart did for his back. We agreed, I would say I was a widow if anyone asked. Yes, I went to see him once or twice, but I never did like to go down to the hospital and Harry didn't want me to see him like that, all wasted away and pale as a ghost. I couldn't take the children in any case, they weren't allowed in.

So, I went to the Corporation, and I told them I was a widow with six children and another on the way. They wouldn't count Fred or Alice as children as such, but they took pity on us. When I said I wanted to keep Ernest and Emily from moving schools again, and I knew there were two empty apartments in Jubilee Square which was closer to George Palmer school than we were in Southampton Street, they agreed.

[I questioned Mrs Hawkins further about what she had said to the Corporation, as it sounded to me as if she had lied for material gain. L.C.]

What was I to do? Stuck in that filthy, stinking place with only Fred's money coming in. I never asked to live in Southampton Street and share a privy with six other families, and I wasn't going to stay if I could get us somewhere else. Harry knew all about it, he agreed it was the best thing for us to do. It was just a pity that Lily never knew her father.

Kitty soon forgot him, and Emily did after a while. I was a widow because Watmore had died. That wasn't a lie, and I'll thank you to make sure you write that down in your fancy shorthand.

We'd had to sell a few things after Harry's accident, so we didn't need a cart to get us into Jubilee Square. Our apartment was two main rooms, a little larger than we'd had at Bedford Court, with a sink and running water in the front room and a little two burner stove in the corner. The back room was a bedroom, and there was a lav. It felt like a palace after Southampton Street. Alice moved back in with us, so we had her wages as well as Fred's to keep us going. There were other children living in the square and Ernest would take his little sisters down to the grass and they would all play together with their skipping ropes and marbles. I could leave the door open and hear them if there was any trouble.

I sent Alice to fetch Mrs Draper when it was my time to have Lily. It should have been like shelling peas by then, she was my nineth after all. But I'd been feeling rough I remember for a few days so I thought it best to have another pair of hands there, and of course I wouldn't need to pay like I would have for a proper midwife. Three days I was in labour. The worst of the lot, Lily was. And when she came out there was hardly anything of her! Mrs Draper thought Lily wouldn't last the night, certainly wouldn't see Christmas, but she did. She was a bit simple, but she survived.

We made that apartment as cosy as we could. Alice got another job in the laundry at the top of Katesgrove Road once I was back on my feet, so she didn't have so far to go every day. And George came home. What a day that was! He'd stayed on in London until the snow had eased off and came to us at the end of January. Fred made up another bed in the front room with him and Ernest. Yes, it was a squeeze, but I wasn't having George stay anywhere else, his home was with us.

He'd grown so tall, taller than Watmore, but he looked every inch his father's son.

He said he'd been in touch with Suttons, and was starting work at one of their nurseries. They had plots of land around the town and more out towards Earley. You know Suttons, don't you? The seed people? George had done some kind of certificate in growing things at his school, and they'd helped him contact Suttons because he'd said he wanted to come back to Reading. Of course, I knew nothing of that then. He hadn't written more than two words in reply to my cards and letters all that time.

I can't say those were bad times at Jubilee Square, though they weren't as good as when we lived in Caversham. There were neighbours to talk to, pals for the children to run about with, and with the three wages we had enough to manage on, more or less. I took in a bit more mending, but with the two girls still not in school there wasn't much I could do. None of us much liked being cooped up in the winter but as soon as the weather improved, we would all be outside in the middle of the square. Us women would bring our chairs out and knit or sew while the children played or slept.

It was mostly women there. Widows like me. Some women who'd been abandoned. Some who'd never got as far as the altar. We all got along alright except for Annie Clarke and Flora ... now what was her last name ... Flora Barclay, that was it. Annie, I didn't mind so much but she used to rub the other women up the wrong way. She'd have men in. Of course we weren't supposed to, it was as against the law then as it is now and just as bad. Now she wasn't one to be hanging around outside pubs in a red shawl or anything like that. She just had her regulars; four or five different men who would come on different days when they finished work or whatever they did in daylight. Annie had twin boys, Terence and Peter; they were a bit younger than Kitty.

Lord knows who their father must have been because Annie had no idea. Those boys were clean and fed, and no one would really have known anything about it except we all saw everything everyone in the square did so it wasn't long before we all knew.

As I say, I didn't mind Annie but her neighbours either side used to say some very spiteful things about her when she wasn't sitting out with us. And Bob Efford who lived in the apartment under Annie's always complained about the noise. How he heard anything I'd like to know; he was as deaf as a post when he wanted to be. And we always thought he rather enjoyed listening, if you know what I mean. I don't know if I should be telling you all this, I don't want to give anyone a bad name or have you think I was a gossip. We just talked amongst ourselves, as you do when you live close together like that.

Flora Barclay was a different kettle of fish altogether. How she ended up in Jubilee Square was a bit of a mystery at first, but I did hear that she'd married a man who'd then committed a terrible crime and who had been sent to prison to do hard labour for twelve years. She'd been disowned by her family and his weren't able to help her much. You could tell she was from good stock, the way she carried herself, the way she spoke with that soft voice of hers and not a hint of harshness about her. But she did look down on the rest of us something terrible.

Flora's little boy was about the same age as Ernest. She wouldn't let William knock about with Ernest though, or any of the other children. We'd see him sometimes at their front window watching the little ones play outside. I used to think that was cruel. Children should be outside when it's good weather, and those apartments were really just for sleeping in, those rooms were small all things considered. Flora would go out all dressed up to the nines in the mornings and then come home with William when he finished school. I did ask her once if she'd like to have William come home with Ernest and Emily, to save her the trip, but you'd think I'd asked if she'd want me to throw William in the river! She looked horrified. I never offered again.

I know a lot more about Flora Barclay now, but it was only after we'd left the square that I found out. The story about her husband was almost true, he had committed a crime and gone to prison, to Reading Gaol down by the Forbury. Nothing violent, which was something I suppose, but he'd been pretending that he owned property and land, selling it to people and taking their money. When the police went to arrest him, he went on the run. It had been in the newspapers, Alice said, but I've never been one for reading newspapers. Anyway, Flora Barclay's husband jumped on a ship and went all the way to Canada, would you believe? They caught him using that fingerprint test or whatever it is. You know, when they make you put ink on your fingers and then onto a bit of paper and then someone says the lines on your fingers matches whatever they think you touched.

They brought him back home to Reading and when they found him guilty, the judge gave him an extra couple of years for running off like that. And do you want to hear the best bit? His father was one of the high-ups in the Reading police! They had already washed their hands of him, which is why they didn't want Flora going round there too much and setting their neighbour's tongues wagging. Her family came from over in Christchurch Gardens, but they had given her a choice of either them or her husband and it was clear which she had chosen. She waited for him mind you. I heard from one of the women at the square that Flora had packed everything up one day and told Gladys that she was going to join her husband and they were all taking a boat to South Africa. Flora said they would be changing their names and making a fresh start where no one knew them. Or what her husband had done, of course. Good luck to them I say. If you get a chance in life like that you should take it.

So, what's all this writing going to do for you, Miss Curtly, if you don't mind my asking?

[I did offer a little information on my plans to complete the journalism course and then find employment in one of our cities. If not London, then perhaps Birmingham or Manchester. Mrs Hawkins seemed genuinely interested that a woman could earn a living by reporting on social issues for magazines and newspapers as I hope to do. L.C.]

Laura investigates

With Mrs Hawkins' tale becoming ever more intriguing, Laura decided she ought to make some attempt to verify the details. It was not an easy task. Despite having approximate dates and locations, and even names in some instances, Laura still felt loath to ask too many questions of her parents. She did not want to alert them to the real nature of her correspondence course until she had fully completed it.

After recovering from the bout of influenza, Laura threw herself on the mercy of A. N. Corley and asked if she might have an extension so as to complete her interviews and submit her final project. The wait for a reply was nerve-wracking and Laura took to walking many miles a day around her local streets so as to avoid accosting the postman each time he passed their house. After a week, she was relieved to have been granted an extra three months at no extra cost.

Laura did manage to surreptitiously extract some information from her parents and two of the schoolmasters with regards to how people could find themselves in a workhouse. Mrs Hawkins' story appeared to be a plausible sequence of events as far as Laura could make out. Gaining a tenancy of a Corporation-owned property was more difficult to establish. Clive was no help in that respect either and it wasn't until Lucy Worthington was again visiting Mrs Curtly that Laura was able to ask her while her mother was momentarily out of the room.

"There is such a need for suitable housing everywhere, my dear. Corporations and local councils do try to provide what they can, but the expense naturally falls to the rate payers and, well, let's just say that a lot of people do not appreciate having to hand over their hard-earned wages to support those who do not also work. They feel it encourages laziness."

"But for women who have very young children, that sort of housing must be of some benefit?"

"Absolutely, but there are always more who need it than is available to them. There are usually committees who must decide who to allocate the accommodation to. They will make inquiries and assess a person's situation. There are rules too. For example, women are often required to not have any further children while they are residing in Corporation housing, or to vacate it if they marry. For many, it really is just one or two steps away from going to the workhouse. Families have been known to send their children away to relatives and then the parents enter the workhouse. I always think that must be so hard on the mother in particular."

"Do you think a woman might do all she could to keep her children with her?"

"Oh yes, undoubtedly. Women in that circumstance are generally fiercely protective of their family. It would be a terrible shame on a woman to have her children taken from her."

This put Mrs Hawkins' lie into perspective for Laura. She was coming to think that despite her hard exterior, Mrs Hawkins did love her children and would not have wanted the shame of entering the workhouse. Harry Jones had done the honourable thing, and Laura decided not to press Mrs Hawkins for further details. Though she had never met him, Laura had developed a soft spot for Harry Jones. He appeared to have been the one good thing that Mrs Hawkins had known up to that point in her life.

Laura decided to take the train to visit Reading and explore some of the locations that Mrs Hawkins had told her about. She also decided not to tell Mrs Hawkins, should the question arise, so that the older lady would not accuse Laura of snooping. Clive had no interest in accompanying Laura, and as none of her other acquaintances knew of her studies, she went by herself.

The town had a reputation for industry, with the Victorian fore-fathers building rows and rows of red-brick housing all around the central commercial area of Broad Street and Friar Street. Here and there, Laura discovered older Georgian-style squares with small communal gardens, but more often she found herself in streets that seemed identical to so many others she had walked along and only the pubs, corner shops and letterboxes aided her navigation.

Mrs Hawkins had been correct in her statement that the courts around St Mary's in the centre of the town had been demolished. This left Laura unable to imagine the squalor of the claustrophobic buildings and the unsanitary conditions that her subject had survived as a child. Jubilee Square however still stood halfway up Silver Street. Laura cautiously spent a few moments looking at the outside of the two-storey apartment blocks. Washing lines were strung across the patch of grass in the centre of the square with laundry flapping in the breeze just as Mrs Hawkins had described it.

Returning to the town centre, Laura took her lunch in Unwin's Café, conscious that years before, Mrs Hawkins and her friend Ada had done just the same. She looked out of the window at the trams and shoppers going about their business. Each one of them has a story, she thought to herself over an egg and cress sandwich. Those stories could be every bit as interesting as Mrs Hawkins', or more so. Laura wanted to know. Why should she struggle to come up with fanciful creative writing as her Mother so expected her to, when real life was right there to be recorded and discussed?

After lunch, Laura's final visit of the day was to the town library. She wanted to see if there were any newspapers for the period that Mrs Hawkins had moved into Jubilee Square, and whether there would be any reports of the criminal trial of Flora Barclay's husband. Laura was nervous in case she was called upon to explain why she wanted to look at the old newspapers, but she need not have been. The librarian was a kindly soul, a woman only a little older than Laura herself, who showed Laura into a reading room and pointed out the long cabinets with wide drawers that held the town's newspapers from earlier that century.

The drawer for 1910 confirmed Mrs Hawkins' tale. Flora Barclay's husband had been charged with forgery and theft, but as he had come from a respectable family (so the newspaper reported) he was allowed bail before his trial at the Crown Court. Laura found the next instalment in a newspaper from the following week, where it was reported that a suspected criminal had absconded and was believed to have left the country bound for the Americas. So absorbed in the drama was Laura that she immediately pulled out the newspapers for the next two weeks. In the second, she discovered a report stating that the police force in Milwaukee, Wisconsin had thought they had apprehended the escapee, but that he had climbed out of a second-storey window only moments before.

It was a newspaper from a fortnight after that Milwaukee report which gave Laura the finale. Flora Barclay's husband was eventually arrested by Canadian police in a boarding house in Toronto. His identity was confirmed by the use of fingerprints, and he was expected to arrive back in Reading to face justice imminently, the report stated. Mrs Hawkins had been correct again. Laura felt somewhat ashamed for doubting the woman, but at the same time satisfied that the newspapers had assisted her in verifying the information. What a worthy resource they were, and she would be proud to provide a similar service one day.

Realising the time, Laura returned the newspapers to their drawer and was not able to establish whether Flora Barclay's husband did indeed receive the sentence that Mrs Hawkins had described. On the train back to London, Laura decided she had no need to question the validity of Mrs Hawkins' information. She had been truthful, and Laura had confidence that should A. N. Corley wish to research any of her submission themselves, they would find it as accurate as could be expected of a memoir of some 20 years ago.

Looking at the faces of her fellow travellers another thought occurred to Laura. She wondered what Flora, Watmore and Mrs Draper had looked like. There had been no illustrations or photographs of Flora's husband in the newspapers. Could Laura describe her subjects sufficiently to allow her readers to form an accurate mental picture? Perhaps she could suggest a camera as her preferred Christmas present from her parents that year.

Interview 4.

[There had been three weeks between our previous interview and this one. I arranged to meet Mrs Hawkins in the public gardens just off the High Street, in the hope that her appetite and the location would not require me to purchase lunch as I had on previous occasions. We began this interview with a resume of Mrs Hawkins' relationship with her children while they were all living at Jubilee Square. L.C.]

Well this is very nice, I must say. Nice to have a change of scene. Are you keeping well? I have been on a little holiday, yes to visit Ada in Newbury. We've kept in touch all these years, and I do like to go over there for a few days every spring. She has a lovely house. Such a pity her John died these 4 years gone now. She's still got the shop though, so a bit of money coming in from that. Her sons have done very well for themselves. Andrew, the eldest, he is a doctor now in Winchester, James their middle one, he has his own fish shop in

Thatcham, and Michael is a manager for the railways in Swindon. Very proud of them is Ada, and so she should be.

You want to know about how things were for my children while we were at Jubilee Square. Well, let me think for a moment. I've got a bag of liquorice here, would you like some?

People say you shouldn't have favourites with your children. I want you to write down that all of my children were wanted, and I tried my best with them all. Like everyone else though, you get along better with some than with others.

Fred was always a bright boy. Watmore would say Fred got his brains and there wasn't much left for the rest of them. We never had any problem getting Fred to school and keeping him there, it was getting him to come home again that was difficult. But give that boy a book or a scrap of newspaper and he'd be happy for hours.

He must have been about four when I found him writing on the wall in the kitchen with a bit of charcoal. He had a page from one of the dailies and was trying to copy the big letters onto the wall. I told him off of course, but I could see he was getting the hang of it, so I sat him at the table with the back of an old cardboard box and his bit of charcoal while I washed the wall down. I said to Watmore later that we needed to get Fred in to school. Watmore didn't hold with schooling, but he knew the truant inspector would be on to us if we didn't send Fred once he was five. And by that time of course, we didn't have to pay for it.

Watmore's friendliness rubbed off on all his children. Fred did well at school, got his certificate and went to work at Huntley and Palmer's like I told you. His pals would call round for him all the time; some would come in for a cup of tea and a chat. They liked to go to the football, or out to play skittles. He was at the biscuit factory a good few years, but all that time he would be going to the talks and taking classes that the social club put on. He was working his way up and could have been management if he'd stayed but he told me just before we left Jubilee Square that he wanted to go to London and try his luck there. I didn't want him to go. You hear such things about London and even though I'd been to Bermondsey that hadn't felt like the city of London as I imagined it then. Fred said George had been telling him about it all and he was sure he could find some work and a room, and he would send money home when he started earning. Well I tried, but I couldn't convince him to stay. He was becoming a man, and with George and Ernest sleeping in the front room it was time for Fred to move on.

He's been settled in Pimlico for years. When he got there, with his letters of recommendation from Huntley and Palmer's, he landed a job at the Aerated Bread Company. He found a room in a house just off Wilton Road. He did well there but he still wanted a better job and a nice house. Who can blame him!

The next thing I heard from him was that he'd joined the Progressive Party. Well, I was surprised as he'd never mentioned politics before, but he said he was to be a secretary for one of the local councillors in Southwark and he would be moving to an apartment above a barber's shop on Borough High Street with a pal he'd got friendly with. Gordon was his name, Gordon Makepeace. Then the war came, and he went off to France. Gordon went too, but never came home again. Funny when you think about it, with a name like Makepeace and all, but there you are. Those poor boys. Fred came back, one of the lucky ones not to lose an arm or a leg. He went back to working for the councillor and then stood in an election himself. He lives in Pimlico again now, in a nice little house, on his own. I've often wondered why he never married, but some men don't, do they.

The war was hard on Alice too. But I'm getting ahead of myself. When we were at Jubilee Square she'd stopped working for a little while when I had Lily and then she got a job with Mary Anne Pocock in her china shop on Silver Street. Mary Anne had the house next to the shop as well and she took in lodgers. Alice stayed there sometimes, but most of the time she came back to Jubilee Square and had her dinner and played with her sisters while I cooked or what have you. Alice was a good girl, hard-working, never complained unlike some I could mention. The only thing we don't see eye to eye on is religion, but that can't be helped.

I think she met David when she was in the shop. It could have been at church though. Alice went to St Giles most Sundays, and sometimes she'd take one or other of Harry's girls but not always. David was a cobbler with a little shop on London Street. They got married just before David went off to France. He never came back either. Alice kept the shop going and took on a young man to work there. She always said it would be just until David came home, but we all knew he was gone for good. No, she never married again. She would take in a lodger now and then, always a young girl mind you. She still lives in London Street above the shop.

Now, George was a changed man when he came back from the Technical School. I've told you how he'd grown so tall, haven't I? He still had his father's temper, the only one of Watmore's children to get that side of him, and I'm thankful for that. But when he came back, he said to me, "Mum, they've had me working outside and I don't know that I can live with an indoor job. So I'll be working at Sutton's nursery in Newtown as a seedman." That school saved George's bacon, I have no doubt whatsoever. When the war started, all the workers at Suttons got exemptions on account of them being so important to the country to feed us all. George volunteered with the fire brigade that Suttons had, but mostly he was out in the trial grounds as they called them in all weathers looking after his plants. He always called them 'his' plants.

George married Louisa; her father worked at Sutton's, and they got to know each other at the social outings they put on for the workers and their families. Suttons was much like Huntley and Palmer's in that respect. Louisa is a lovely girl; I've always been very fond of her. They have a nice house on Foxhill Road and George grows the biggest dahlias you ever saw! Huge like dinner plates they are, and all different colours. They're his pride and joy, and you'd think he'd want to put his feet up after being outside all day, but he spends just as much time in his greenhouse at home as he does at work.

Yes, they have two children. Malcolm is at the University, he is studying history though I don't know what use that will be to him. Jane is at school and wants to be a hairdresser. Such a lovely little family.

You know, they have a little café on the other side of this park. I'm that parched with all this talking. Why don't we have a cup of tea and I'll tell you about Ernest.

I suppose some people would have liked Ernest the best out of Watmore's children. He was never as confident as Fred, but he had the same intelligence. Ernest has never had much drive though; he's never wanted to better himself as some would. When we lived in Caversham, he adored that little dog, Jack. He'd spend hours in the garden rolling around with that dog, and he'd tie a bit of string around Jack's neck and lead him around the garden. He'd bring in birds that had been mauled by cats, beetles and goodness knows what else in jam jars, and he once kept a toad in a cardboard box for a week before I found it and made him set the poor thing free. He wanted Harry and Fred to dig a pond in the garden at Albert Road, but they wouldn't because we needed to grow vegetables.

Ernest was never particularly keen on the bigger animals. He liked to sit on Dolly, all the children did, but he was never as involved with her as Fred was. I did think for a while that Ernest might end up at the cattle market or somewhere like that, but Ernest had as much of Watmore's luck as George did. His teacher at George Palmer school set Ernest up with a friend of his who had a pig farm in Whitley. Ernest would ride his bicycle over there on Saturdays and help the farmer, and then when he finished school, he went to work there every day, still riding his bicycle there and back. Do you know, I don't remember where that bicycle came from. Gawd, I hope those boys didn't pinch it!

He married a girl called Charlotte, they're living now on Elgar Road. They had a little girl, Josie. Always was a sickly child, something not right with her heart so they say. He doesn't still ride the bicycle, no, he's got a motorcycle now with a funny name; Bruff or Matches, something like that.

[I believe the motorcycle to be either a Brough Superior or a Matchless model. L.C.]

Harry's girls are out working, and Lily is married. Emily and Kitty live together. Emily is a teacher at George Palmer school and Kitty works at the telephone exchange. No, they never married, although Emily was seeing a young chap, Arthur, for a while but he was another one who went off to war and never came back again. They've got a nice little house at the top of Northumberland Avenue, nice garden at the back with a bit of grass and some flowers.

Lily worked at the University, Wantage Hall, as a service girl before she married Ron. I mentioned she was a bit slow, didn't I? And always eating, that girl! She'd finish up anything the other girls left, not that there was ever much left on my children's plates, you can be sure of that. Emily had to let Lily's work uniform out a couple of times, and I did ask her if there was anything I should know, but she didn't have any idea what I was on about and thankfully it didn't seem like there was. Now Lily and Ron met at St Giles, and that's where they got married in twenty-nine. Ron was teaching the Sunday School and he would sing in the choir. Lily couldn't hold a note in a bucket, but Ron has a lovely voice. Quiet man, lost his brother in the war. He's a handyman down at the sewerage works at the bottom of Basingstoke Road. That's not too far from where Ernest works, and Ron's parents live in Elgar Road as well. It's a small world, don't you agree? Oh yes, Lily and Ron live behind George Palmer school, on Surrey Road.

[I asked what Mrs Hawkins had worn to her children's weddings, and her reply shocked me once again. L.C.]

Oh, I never went to them. No, well, I had the girls at home still when George and Louisa got married. And then I was in Newbury when Ernest married Charlotte, and by the time Lily married Ron I was here in London. Yes, because by then you see I'd married Albert North.

Now we're getting all out of order here. Yes, Harry died in the workhouse in nineteen-twelve, so I really was a widow again for a second time, and with his three girls on top of Watmore's children. We'd had no chance to save or anything like that, though I did get a few pounds from the Dairy when Harry got run over, but only enough to bury him with. I would go down and see him while he was in the hospital but that stopped when he went into the workhouse. They would put the workhouse deaths in the newspaper and Alice read it out to me one day. So that was that with Harry.

I was down in the dumps for a bit, I don't mind telling you. I couldn't see how we'd manage once Alice got herself married, not if Fred settled elsewhere. Then George came home and everything was alright for a while with his money coming in. I did a bit of cleaning at the Coach and Horseshoes at the top of Silver Street, early in the morning so I could take Lily with me, and Alice would get the others off to school and leave Kitty with one of the neighbours until I got home again. They asked me if I'd work behind the bar, but I had to say no. I didn't want a reputation like Annie Clarke, and everyone knows what goes on when women work in pubs. Not when they own pubs, no, don't get me wrong there. Mrs Graham never kept a bawdy house at the Red Cow, but some of the pubs closer to town were well known for getting the barmaids to work extra upstairs or in the back room.

The Coach and Horseshoes was at the end of Whitley Parade, that's a row of shops with rooms above for the shop owners to live in. There was a fruit and veg shop next to the pub and they were having an extra room built on to the back of their shop, a storeroom for the veg I suppose. The builders would be there working when I came out of the back gate of the pub and I'd pass the time of day with them as you do, to be polite. One of them seemed to be in charge, and always had stopped for a mug of tea when I finished so we'd have a bit of a chat. Unless it was raining, or Lily was crying for something to eat. I got to know Bert North that way. He had a house on Alpine Street and lived there with his mother. She was a widow like me, Bert's father had died years ago, on the railway he said.

One day, when they had almost finished the building work, he asked if he might walk me home. He said the other men could finish up and he knew by then that I didn't live more than five minutes down the street. I thought nothing of it at the time. Lily was just about able to walk then, so I'd been thinking I'd need to start leaving her with Alice in the mornings if I wanted to keep doing the cleaning job. Bert took one look at Jubilee Square and he said to me, "We can do better than this, my girl!"

I asked him what he meant, and he said, "When we're married, you'll come and live at Alpine Street, there's plenty of room." And that was it. No proposal so to speak, he'd just made up his mind and that was that. He always was a decisive man. I liked that about him. What I didn't know then was he wanted someone to keep an eye on his mother. She'd taken to wandering when she was left on her own. Bert being her only son at home, he couldn't look after her because he had to work so he'd taken to locking her in the house while he was out. He didn't like it, he worried she'd burn the house down and her with it, so he'd pop back two or three times during the day to make sure she was alright.

No, my mother had died by then. Did I miss that bit out? Yes, she passed away when we were living in Caversham. Father was paying off the funeral a bit each week, and a bit extra to cover his own when the time came. I did ask him if he wanted to come in with us somewhere when we had to move back to town. He said he didn't want to leave West Court, he'd been there so long; he knew everyone and everyone knew him. It was a good job that he was paying that extra couple of bob a week for his own casket because he died just a short while after Bert North said we'd be getting married.

I suppose that's what convinced me to marry him. Bert paid for Father's funeral. Nothing fancy, but just topped up what was owed for the plot and coffin. I did go to Father's funeral; he was laid next to Mother out at Cemetery Junction. Alice came, but none of the others. Funerals are no place for small children, and besides, the boys were all working. Then not six weeks later, Bert and I were married at St Giles on a Tuesday afternoon. We had sandwiches and a couple of pints of beer at the Coach and Horseshoes while his workmates moved all my belongings out of Jubilee Square and into Alpine Street for us.

We had more room there, certainly. The house is in a terrace with three floors. You go straight into the front room, the stairs go up the middle of the house, and the kitchen is at the back with a lav in the back yard. Bert always said he'd build one onto the back of the kitchen, but he never did. We had the front bedroom, the girls were in the back and Granny North was in the attic.

I fell for Violet straight away. Nine months to the day after our wedding she was born. Bert was over the moon when I told him. He'd wanted children for a long time you see, but having never been married until I came along, he thought he'd missed the boat. How old was I? Forty-two when I had Vi, and forty-four when I had James. I said no more after James and I stuck to my guns. But don't let me get ahead of myself again, else none of this will make sense.

Alpine Street wasn't a patch on our house in Caversham, but Bert's dad had bought it so at least we didn't have to find rent money. That was a weight off all our minds, I can tell you. We'd become dab hands at lying low when the rent man came calling, and it was nice not to have that worry anymore. For a while at least things were good between Bert and me. He took the girls in as if they were his own, never played favourites. George would visit every Sunday for his dinner and Alice was still with us then. Bert was too old to go off to war, so I had that to be thankful for as well. He was working hard and started doing jobs on the side at weekends to earn a bit more. At least, that's what he told me.

Then the War started. George would have gone, he wanted to, but he wasn't allowed. His foreman said he'd lose his job if he did, and that feeding the nation was more important in the long run. Ernest wasn't quite old enough at the start, and then the farmer got him an exemption on account of Ernest being the only one there looking after the pigs and the farmer being ill. I can't say I was sad about that. Ernest wouldn't have liked the army life. He and George were so different, you wouldn't think they had the same father. Fred went off almost straight away though, with Gordon. He didn't meet Vi until he had a bit of home leave just after James was born.

Fred missed Alice's wedding too. She married David when I was pregnant with Vi, and David was gone two days later. Handed Alice the keys to his shop and the rooms above in London Street and never came home again. Missing in action, the telegram said. Alice took it badly at first. She came hammering on our front door sobbing her heart out. I sat her down, gave her a drop of brandy, and then after a few minutes I had to tell her to pull herself together as she was upsetting the girls. I said to her, you've got a home and the shop, there's plenty worse off than you, my girl.

George stayed with Alice for a while then, just to have a man about the place and make sure the shop stayed open. He helped her find Johnny, the young man who runs the shop now. He'd been apprenticed to a bootmaker in Friar Street and had been looking for a place to start his own business, but George convinced Johnny that taking on Alice and David's shop would be just as good with not as much risk. George was always good at talking people into things, just like his father. Johnny's still there, yes. Didn't I say? He's deaf, that's why he didn't go to war. He wasn't born that way, no, but he had measles when he was a boy and lost most of his hearing then. He watches what people say and reads their lips, so Alice tells me.

Yes, I was luckier than many, I know that. Mrs Thomas in Jubilee Square lost five of her grandsons. Lizzy Mason lost all three of her sons. Nelly O'Shea who lived next to us in Bedford Court lost two sons and the other who did come back lost his leg and most of his senses.

Shell shock they call it, you know. She'd find him on the floor most mornings she said, shaking like a leaf and couldn't get him up without her husband's help. Fred doesn't talk about it, and I never asked him. It doesn't do to dwell on the past; it's not as if you can change any of it.

Well look at the time! I need to do a bit of shopping and get back home, so if that's enough for today I'll be on my way. Hang on, I've got tuppence for my tea in here somewhere. There you are. Same time next week, shall we say?

Laura has a revelation

As Laura read back through her hasty shorthand, it struck her that Mrs Hawkins, and her family, had experienced so much death in their lives – certainly more than Laura herself had known. She had no siblings, so the prospect of seeing one die was thankfully impossible. Had that first experience and the way the adults around her behaved, instilled the almost off-hand manner with which Mrs Hawkins now described death?

Laura wondered for the first time how she would react to either of her parents' deaths. She had never known her grandparents, so no experience was to be found there. She had, she realised, never attended a funeral. Laura tried to think back over the years to identify any funerals her parents had been to. She thought her father might have been to one for his old school master, but she couldn't be sure. Her own circle of acquaintances was small, mostly girls of her own age and their mothers, though occasionally she would hear that someone in the village had passed on. Perhaps her parents had been to many funerals, yet had simply never mentioned them in her hearing.

There would not have been as many funerals during the War as one might expect, Laura conceded. As Mrs Hawkins had commented several times, so many of the men who went to fight never returned at all. Laura passed the memorial in the village regularly but had never really looked at the names inscribed on it. In fact, her only real interest in it had up until now been when the poppy garlands had begun to wither at its base and make the street look rather shabby.

Laura put her notes to one side, put on her coat and hat, and set out for the memorial. She felt a need to read those names, to see which families in the village had lost sons and brothers. The afternoon was overcast and blustery. Puddles reflected the scurrying, inky clouds above. Laura walked with purpose, her head up and alert. It took only a few minutes for her to reach the grey monolith, and as she did so the clouds parted briefly and allowed a shaft of sunlight to rain down on the memorial before her. She read the names, starting at the top left with Abel and Adderley. There were two Fishers, two Landrys and three Mercers. In all, twenty-eight names ending with T. M. York. Laura wondered how many of them had returned home. She would look in the churchyard.

It was a well-tended plot. The Sexton took great pride in his clipped hedges and trimmed grass edges. The gravel crunched under Laura's shoes as she strode towards the rear of the church where the newer graves were located. She realised she was hoping to see rows of identical headstones, the familiar Portland stone markers with the names she had just read on the memorial. Clive had mentioned recently how there were some 60,000 war graves across the country, surely she would find some there in her little village.

As Laura turned the corner of the end of the church, it was clear that not all twenty-eight men from the memorial had been buried there. She scanned the rows as she walked, slower now as she approached the newer part of the churchyard. Ahead she could see three Portland headstones, but one large gravestone in polished pink granite caught her eye to her right. The name Landry was repeated again and again from top to bottom:

'William Landry, born 1853, died 1897. His wife Elizabeth Landry, born 1854, died 1888. Their son Alfred Landry, born 1875, died 1916. Thomas Landry, son of Alfred, born 1899, died in France in 1916. Michael Landry, son of Alfred, born 1900, died in Belgium in 1917. Constance Landry, daughter of Alfred, born 1903, died 1912. Thy will be done.'

Laura stood for a moment and read the names, following the family down through the generations. Where was Alfred's wife, she wondered. How had she born the loss of her three children (had there been more Landry children?) and her husband? Had she too become accepting of the recurring event, just as one might accept that today was cloudy when yesterday had been brilliantly sunny, and knowing that eventually the sun would return. Yet dead relatives did not return. How did anyone bare it, Laura wondered.

She moved on, now at the last three rows of graves, and to where the three pale markers were arranged together. Like soldiers on parade, Laura thought sadly. Here were Privates Abel and Connor, and Lieutenant Rook. At the base of Private Connor's headstone, someone had left a jam jar with now wilted carnations. Someone remembered him. Was it family? A sweetheart as Mrs Hawkins' daughters Alice and Emily had been? Perhaps a teacher who remembered a bright young boy full of life and potential.

Laura did not linger at the graves; she felt as if she were a tourist, feeding on the misfortune of others. She made her way back towards the churchyard gate but stopped by a bench and sat down. Struck by an almost overwhelming feeling of needing to know all about the

Landrys, the other lost soldiers, all of Mrs Hawkins' family, Laura's neighbours in the village, Clive's school and university chums ... everyone; Laura's heart was beating faster in her chest. Everyone deserved to be known, she decided. No one should be allowed to slip away through history as if they had never been. She might not be able to help them in any material way if they suffered hardship or indignity, but she could tell the world that they had existed.

Interview 5.

[I had felt there was something Mrs Hawkins had been reluctant to tell me about her relationship with her third husband during our previous interview. She had been trying to make light of their living arrangements with her elderly mother-in-law, so when we met again, I decided to press her for more details. L.C.]

Her name was Dorothy. Bert called her Mum of course, but I never could bring myself to do that, so she was always Granny North to me and the children. I did my best by her for as long as I could, you write that down. I tried. But she wasn't my mother, and I was getting on myself, what with having Vi and then James as well as Harry's girls, even with Alice's help it was a lot to take on. Some people say it's like having another child, but I can tell you, Granny North was more hard work than any of my children.

It's not a job for a man. A man doesn't want to be feeding and washing his own mother. By the end of our first week of marriage I could see exactly why Bert had wanted me to move in there with them, and Harry's girls were a price he was willing to pay just to have someone else look after his mum. Don't get me wrong, I liked Bert and Bert liked me. I don't think he'd have married just anyone. But once I was there, he was able to spend a bit more time out working, or so he told me.

Granny North didn't sleep much. We'd been at Alpine Street a couple of weeks, and I woke up in the night because I needed the lav. I was coming back up the stairs and I could see the girl's room door was open. I looked in and Granny North was standing by Emily and Kitty's bed. Well, that gave me a funny feeling. She wasn't doing anything, she was just standing there in her nightdress looking at them, but I didn't like it. I spoke to Bert about it, and he agreed we could bolt Granny North's door again at night. She had a commode, not that she always used it, so she didn't need to go downstairs. For a while she would bang on the door and wake us all up, and then she would start wailing, but she stopped eventually. I just wasn't happy with her wandering around at night.

The further along I was with Vi, the more difficult Granny North became. She kept wanting to touch my stomach, especially when I was trying to feed her or wash her or get her dressed. Lily had started at George Palmer school by then at the nursery class, and I didn't tell Bert, but I would sometimes lock Granny North in her room for an hour or so in the day, just so I could have a bit of rest by myself. Those were a strange few months; it was the first time since I'd had Fred where there were no children in the house during the day. If Granny North hadn't been there, I would have been a real lady of leisure as they say.

I could have put my feet up and rested after lunch if I'd wanted, like they tell the young girls to these days.

There was so much washing to do though, that's what I spent most of my time doing as I remember. Keeping Harry's girls' pinafores clean for school, Bert's clothes were always dirty and sweaty from the bricklaying, and Granny North's bedding never lasted more than a couple of days before it needed changing. I was grateful for the line in the back yard, but in the winter we had to string one up in the kitchen as well as the airer to try and get things dry.

Granny North had to stay with us, it was her house. It only went to Bert when she died and that was only a couple of years ago. The closer I got to having Vi, the more worried I was about having her with Granny North around. I thought it would be just my luck that Granny North would fall down the stairs or set the kitchen alight while I was in the middle of giving birth. I spoke to Bert about it, but he wasn't worried. He said we'd just lock Granny North in her room as usual, but I told him if the doctor had to come out and found her locked up, we'd have hell to pay!

We didn't have any other rooms for anyone else to stay with us, so in the end I wrote to Minnie Draper, or Armitage as she was by then. You remember I said she'd moved away to London? She'd married Frank Armitage and had another little girl after the one she left with her mother. They had a hat shop in Hackney, Frank was a hatter as well, and as Alice was in no state to help me, I asked Minnie if I might stay with them for my confinement. We'd kept in touch on and off, not quite as regular as I had with Ada, but often enough to still say we were friends.

No, I couldn't go to Ada's then because she was already looking after John's mother. They'd had her move in with them a year or so before when John's father had died. That's how they came to have their nice house you see; they went in together and bought it between them. John's mother wasn't batty like Granny North though, Ada was lucky in that respect too.

So anyway, I said to Bert I was going off to London to have the baby and he'd have to see to his mother himself for a couple of weeks. He wasn't happy about it. He wanted me to take Harry's girls with me, but I said Emily was old enough to see to them all and he'd only have to make sure there was food in the house for them. Emily was eleven, nearly twelve then. I did think about taking Lily with me but in the end I only had enough for my train ticket, and she was so happy to be at school like her sisters. I didn't want to have to deal with the truant inspector on top of everything else.

Yes, that was a very strange time. I'd only been at Minnie and Frank's for two days when I had Vi. Out she popped, dear little thing, easy as anything. Minnie had a midwife come round and see that everything was alright, no fever or anything like that. I felt like a queen those few days I can tell you. Tucked up in bed with Vi sleeping and feeding well, all my meals done for me, all my washing too. The house was quiet, but I had the window open in my room and I could hear the birds singing outside. I remember that clear as anything. The birds and whistles from the trains every now and then. I told Minnie if there was ever anything I could do for her, to pay her and Frank back, she was to tell me straight away. I didn't really want to leave, and I suppose that was what gave me the idea to ... well, we'll get to that later.

I did leave, of course. I registered Vi's birth in Hackney and then when she was 12 days old, I went back to Reading. Everyone was so pleased to see me! The girls had picked some flowers from some-where and they were in a milk bottle on the kitchen table. Emily had scrubbed the kitchen and tried to do the laundry but she couldn't get any of it through the mangle so it was all dripping out in the yard. I remember Granny North was very quiet the first few days I was back, almost like she'd forgotten who I was and didn't know what to make of me, or Vi. I was very careful not to leave Vi if Granny North wasn't in her room. The girls all loved Vi and Lily wanted to take her out in their old pram. So I said we'd all go out the next morning and I'd walk with the girls to school. I hadn't done that in a long time and they were all so excited about it. I did their hair with ribbons and they all had clean pinafores on, and everyone we passed was saying 'Good day,' to us and the girls were telling everyone they had a new baby sister.

I remember when we got to the school, Kitty asked me if Auntie Edith would be coming for her dinner again. I didn't know any Auntie Edith, so I told her not to be so silly and to get off into school. But it made me think. Then a day or so later when we were all having our dinner, Lily asked the same thing, but she asked Bert. His face was a picture. He went bright red, and I thought he was going to drop down on the floor right there and then with his heart! I wasn't stupid. I knew what it all meant. I wasn't going to start a row with the girls there though, so I waited until we'd finished eating and then I sent them out to play in the yard. Bert knew what was coming and he'd had time to think of a reason.

He said he'd needed some help with Granny North and a woman down the street he'd known for years had offered to come round and see to her. See to him, more like! He said she'd stayed for her dinner so that she could get Granny North back into bed afterwards. I could tell whose bed she'd been interested in. I told him, that woman was never to cross our threshold again while I was in that house. I was angry, not because he'd been fooling around with another woman, but that he'd done it right there in my house.

[I reminded Mrs Hawkins that it was still the elder Mrs North's house at that time. L.C.]

In name, yes. By the law, yes. But who kept it clean? Who made sure the fires were stoked and the yard swept? Who scrubbed the front step every Monday morning? That was my house as much as anyone's and I wasn't having some tart sneaking in as soon as my back was turned.

Bert agreed. He said he'd been foolish and should have known what would happen. He promised it wouldn't happen again. Of course I didn't believe him but we got along together and he'd taken in Harry's girls, and now we had Vi as well, so I let the matter drop. I think Bert did stop seeing that Edith for a while at least. He didn't take on as much extra work as he had been. He didn't pay as much attention to Vi as Harry had to his girls, but they were very different men. Bert was a man's man, if you know what I mean. Always happier when he was with his pals or working.

We rubbed along as we had been for a year or so and then I fell pregnant with James. That was the worst pregnancy of the lot! I was so sick, morning noon and night for weeks. Just getting out of bed in the morning would set me off retching. Emily had to do most of the cooking as I couldn't stand to smell raw meat. It was a good thing she was almost at the end of her schooling, though she wanted to go to a teacher training school afterwards. We couldn't afford it, but she said she would get a job and save up for it herself, and she did. It took her three years working in Huntley and Palmer's but she saved half of her wages every week and went off to be a teacher. She was always good with the children, just like Alice was.

I'll be honest with you, I thought I was too old to be having any more children and Bert definitely was. I was forty-four and Bert was fifty-one, and we hadn't been exactly careful if you know what I mean.

So, while James was wanted, he certainly wasn't planned. When I started to get bigger, Granny North's old tricks began again, and I told Bert I wasn't having any of it that time. I told him, "I'm going to write to Minnie again and stay with her when my time comes."

I said I'd take Vi with me, she was too small to leave by herself with Emily. I'd more or less forgotten about that Edith he'd had in the last time, and I didn't think he'd be so stupid as to do the same thing again. Have you got a young man? Yes, well, don't you believe him if he tells you there's no one else. They're all as bad as each other, though I don't believe Harry ever did anything like that.

Off I went again to Hackney. I must have got my dates muddled because I ended up staying there for nearly a month. Minnie and Frank were very good about it. They were doing very well for themselves, and Minnie's daughter Thomasina was working with them as a milliner. That was when I found out where Thomasina's name had come from.

Minnie and Frank's house has a little garden out back, not a yard like the one in Alpine Street but a bit of grass and some veg that Frank put in. Thomasina was out there with Vi, and me and Minnie were watching them through the parlour window. We got talking about baby names, and I asked why she'd chosen Thomasina. She went all quiet and then she said the girl was named after her father. Now, you'll remember I said that when Minnie was pregnant with her, she wouldn't tell a soul who the father was. And you might remember that Watmore's name was Thomas.

Yes, I can see you've worked it out about as fast as I did. We were both quiet for a while, just sitting there watching the girls in the garden. Then Minnie reached over and took hold of my hand on the table and said she was very sorry. She said she had never told anyone else, not even Frank, but it was such a secret to carry, and she hoped I would understand that it was just a couple of times that she'd been with Watmore. It was all water under the bridge, I said. I couldn't be angry with her, not after all that time. Watmore was a handsome man, I knew other girls looked at him and I had an idea he went with a few on and off. They all do. I could see Watmore in Thomasina, I just hadn't realised it until then. She was tall and dark, and friendly in her ways, and really would have passed as a full sister to Alice rather than a half sister. Funny that I hadn't wondered about it all when I'd been there to have Vi really, but there you are.

Minnie and Frank's other daughter is a tiny blonde thing, with a twisted leg and her hand is like a claw. She'd had the cord around her neck when she was born and they thought she wouldn't live long, but she was stronger than she looked. Imogen they called her, Immy. She didn't go to school until she was seven or eight, and she needn't have gone then because she was an invalid, but Minnie and Frank wanted her to have some friends and to see if she could learn a few things. Immy won't work, that's for certain. She can't hold things with her bad hand. She seems happy enough at home with Minnie though, and Thomasina adores her, that's plain to see.

James was a difficult birth. Really he couldn't have been less like Vi, and even now you wouldn't think they were brother and sister. They are though, before you go getting any ideas. The men might wander but I've always been faithful when I've been married. You write that down. I was in labour for nearly three days. It was just like having Fred all over again, but at least I knew with James what was meant to be happening. I kept telling Minnie not to get the midwife in too early, I could feel that it was going to be a long time. I was so tired by the time the midwife did come, she had me lay on the bed and said she'd only make me get up again if it looked like the baby was stuck.

James was such a big boy. Eight pounds and an ounce he was. I couldn't believe it when the midwife told me; all the others had been six pounds or less. He was a bit yellow, jaundice they call it, a few days after he was born but the midwife said there was nothing to worry about. It wasn't quite the same as before when it had just been me and Vi. This time Vi was two and sleeping in the room with me, so every time James woke up, Vi did as well. I had a big pram then, Bert brought it home after I'd gone back with Vi, I think as a peace offering. It meant I could get us all safely back to Reading on the train when I was ready to leave Hackney.

It was Granny North who told me that time. Bert had been so careful not to let the girls see that woman, Edith, after Kitty and Lily had given the game away before. He waited until the girls had gone to bed and then put a light on in our front bedroom window so that Edith would know she could go round. She only lived at the bottom of Alpine Street you see, with her brother and his family after her husband had thrown her out. But Bert still wanted someone to put Granny North to bed so he couldn't hide Edith from her.

I'd been back at Alpine Street for about a week with James, and Vi was teething. Granny North called me Edith. She'd never called me anything before, but I was washing her one morning and she didn't want to be washed. She started shouting, "No, Edith, no!" and trying to push my hands away. I ignored her and finished what I had to do, and she calmed down in the end. Then she did the same thing that evening when I was getting her ready for bed. Bert heard her, and by the time I'd finished with Granny North he had his story ready again.

He'd only asked Edith to see to his mother, he said. Nothing funny had gone on between them that time. He swore on James' life, but I was so angry it didn't make any difference. I don't know what came over me. I was tired of it all I suppose, being taken for granted and for a fool. I threw Granny North's chamber pot at Bert and told him he could see to her from then on. It smashed on the wall behind him, but

I was already halfway down the stairs by then. I went out of the house and down the street to where Edith lived. I banged on their door and started shouting for her to show her face. There were lights going on in all their neighbours' houses but I didn't care. Her brother opened the door, and I could see Edith behind him, so I made to grab for her to drag her outside. I missed, and her brother pushed me back off their doorstep, and Bert had caught up with me by then and was trying to calm me down. That only made things worse.

I was screaming at her, I'm ashamed to say now. I don't know as that I want you to write this, but I'll tell you anyway. Bert was trying to pull me back to our house, but I turned on him and punched him right on his nose. It started pouring with blood, I think I might have broken it, I certainly hurt my hand, not that I cared just then. I shouted at Edith that if she liked it inside my house so much, she could move in and look after the whole bloody lot! Then I marched back up the street and back into our house. I slammed the door and Bert didn't have his key, so he was hammering on our door and waking our neighbours too. Emily woke up and came to the top of the stairs while I was in the bedroom packing my clothes. I told her I was going away for a while and that she needed to be a good girl and look after her brother and sisters for me.

I did think about taking James. I really did. But in that moment, I didn't want anything to do with Bert, and James was part of him. I went down to the kitchen and took the housekeeping money from the tin on the dresser, put my coat on and went out through the back gate into the alley and down behind the houses to Elgar Road. I could hear everyone in the street shouting. I suppose Bert must have eventually gone round to the alley and let himself in through the back door the same way I'd left, unless Emily let him in the front, but I didn't care. I walked into town to the train station and bought a ticket to London.

Interview 5 continued.

I'm not proud of what I did, leaving the children. I mean, what kind of woman does that to her own flesh and blood? That's what people ask, isn't it. Minnie and Frank know of course, and so does Ada, but no one else who knows me now, knows my life before I came back to London. They all think I'm a widow, which I am, though just not recently. The only reason I agreed to tell you all this was because you said you wouldn't use everyone else's real names. No one will know it's me or recognise themselves, you said.

[I reassured Mrs Hawkins at this point that her confidentiality was absolute, and then had to explain what that meant. She was then willing to continue. L.C.]

It was almost midnight when I got off the train. I couldn't go waking Minnie and Frank up and I didn't want to spend money on a taxi to Hackney in any case, so I found a small church near the station and stayed there that night. I slept on the floor, wrapped up in my coat with one of the kneelers as a pillow. I was lucky that the door was open, thinking about it now. So much thieving around these days, the vicars don't like to leave the churches unlocked, do they.

It's strange, the things you remember and the things you forget. It was October, and the wind was so cold. I don't remember anything about the train ride, but I remember the wind as I crossed the road outside the station. I remember sleeping until it was daylight again. I hadn't slept that long in so many years even though the floor was cold and hard. I sat up and the first thing I saw was my case on the floor with everything I owned in it. It was real then. I'd left Bert, left the children, though I told myself then that I'd go back for them, and left Reading. I was forty-five and on my own for the first time ever.

I remember counting out the money I had on one of the pews. It wasn't a lot, and it wouldn't last more than a week or so even if I only ate one meal a day. I gave myself a good talking to, I can tell you. I had to find a job and somewhere to sleep. I decided having somewhere to sleep was the most important thing, so I set off to Hackney. I needed to get going before the vicar found me and started asking questions in any case; I didn't want to have to tell a stranger what I'd done. I explained everything to Minnie and Frank when I got to their house though, and they were as good as gold to me. They let me stay, and I wrote to Fred to ask him if he still had his apartment, and could I stay there while he was in France. He'd had to let it go, so that was no good, but he said I should go and see the lady who he'd rented it from as she had several properties, and one might be available.

I couldn't afford the one place that she had. It was lovely; looked out onto a park and had an indoor lav, but I hadn't got a job and I heard Harry's voice in my head warning me not to take on more than I could afford. She even offered to lower the rent a bit on account of me knowing Fred, but it was still too much. She was a nice lady. I wonder what happened to her.

I had better luck finding a job. They'd just opened the big munitions factory on Hackney Marshes and they wanted women to put the shells together there so I went over to see what it was all about. All the girls were so much younger than me and all keen to do their bit for the war. That never occurred to me you know; I just needed a job so I could find a place of my own to live. I had an interview with a manager in a suit and a bow tie, and he said I could have a job as a cook in their canteen. I was happy with that. The canaries – that's what the girls were called, you know; the chemicals turned their skin yellow after a while – their jobs were dangerous. It only took someone dropping one of those shells and the whole place would go up. I was happy working in the kitchens and that's where I met your mother's friend Lucy Parks, or Worthington as she is now. You see, I said it was a small world, didn't I?

I didn't write to Watmore's children, apart from Fred of course, until I was settled at the boarding house. I could have stayed with Minnie and Frank, but I didn't want to impose on them, and they were busy with the shop and with Immy. They have been very good to me over the years though. I stayed a few weeks, just to get a bit of money in my pocket to set me up, and then I moved into a room in Kingsland. It was a bit of a walk to the factory and back every day, but several of the girls lived nearby and we'd all walk together.

Alice wrote to me almost as soon as she must have got my letter to her. She said she had already heard about me shouting in the street and Bert was telling everyone that I'd be back with my tail between my legs. I think his pride was hurt more than his nose. Alice wanted me to go back, for the sake of the children she said. But how could I? With everyone in Alpine Street knowing my business, knowing what

Bert had been up to with that Edith, and knowing I'd left my children there even for a couple of weeks as it had been then. I know what they'd think even if they didn't say it. What kind of woman leaves her children behind? It wasn't as if I had been in any danger, Bert never lifted a finger towards me though he swore often enough.

I tried to explain it to Alice when I wrote back to her, but how do you explain to a young girl whose husband has been most likely killed that you just didn't want to stay with your own anymore? That you were tired of always having a baby at your breast and a crowd of them around your feet, when that young girl won't have a chance of children? I was selfish, and that's what everyone would think of me. In the end I said I thought I'd had some kind of fit of hysteria and when I felt better, I would see if Harry's girls would want to come to me. What else could I say?

I stayed at that boarding house in Kingsland for about a year. There were a couple of other girls from the factory staying there as well, and we looked out for each other. I suppose they thought of me as a sort of mother figure, which is funny really seeing as that's what I'd wanted to get away from. It was like being back in Jubilee Square, just without the children all around. We'd sit in the park at the end of the street on sunny evenings and the girls would smoke and we'd have a natter. I never smoked, no. We weren't allowed to in the boarding house, so the girls would hang out of their windows and blow the smoke outside. I worked six days a week in the kitchens. Even though it was a factory, it was very different to working at Huntly and Palmer's. Not so strict for a start; the girls could chat as long as they didn't stop what they were doing. There were some men working there as well, but mostly it was women in the assembly and packing rooms.

I remember we were coming home one Saturday and there was a big crowd outside the little Quaker chapel in Kingsland. We asked some people what was going on and they said there was a pacifists' meeting inside and the crowd were going to drag them out! We went along to watch and some of the girls were frightened. The men were hammering on the door of the chapel, and then one climbed up and began kicking at one of the windows. He put his foot right through it and then him and another chap pulled at the leading and glass and made the hole big enough to get through. It must have been a fair drop down on the other side though because they didn't climb inside. Instead, they started throwing bricks and all sorts through the window at the people inside.

There was a policeman there on his horse, but he only hung around for a minute or two and then carried on his way. Everyone was shouting at the men inside, calling them cowards and, 'Shame! Shame!' We heard one man say they should burn the chapel down and we left then because we didn't want to get mixed up in any trouble like that.

Did you want to know about the influenza? I'd moved to Haggerston by then.

[I asked if she might say how her other children had reacted to Mrs Hawkins flight to London first. It seemed odd that she had only mentioned her daughter Alice. L.C.]

I didn't hear much from Fred, he was always moving from one place to another with the army and it sometimes took weeks for letters to arrive. He'd met Bert of course, but he'd never had much to do with him. He did ask if Bert had been rough with me, but I put him straight on that account. Fred said if he had a chance he'd go and visit the next time he was in Reading, to see how Harry's girls were doing. He's always been a good boy. He went and saw them, met Vi and James while he was there, and told Bert that I was in London, but he wouldn't give him my address. Fred told me later that Bert said he hadn't moved Edith in to replace me, and Emily confirmed it when Fred asked her. I suppose she hadn't really wanted all Bert had to offer after all. Bert had found a wet nurse for James, a woman in Elgar Road had lost her baby and took James in. He stayed with that lady until he was almost a year old and then went back to Alpine Street and Kitty looked after him and Vi.

It was Louisa who wrote to me to say George would have had me stay with them if he'd known. He hadn't taken to Bert any more than he had to Harry, which surprised me really because Bert was much more like Watmore. George was never close to Harry's girls, what with him being away at school, so I never expected he would look out for them. I've been to visit him and his little family two or three times; it's easier to stay with them than with Alice and nothing is ever too much trouble for Louisa. Lovely girl, she is.

Ernest brought Charlotte over to George's house once when I was visiting but I haven't seen them since. Now they live on Elgar Road, it's a bit too close for comfort if you know what I mean. The last thing I want to do is run into Bert or Edith, or any of my old neighbours for that matter. Ernest was upset about it all. He was always a sensitive lad, and Charlotte said Harry's girls could live with them if they wanted to, even with Josie being sickly. There was a bit of an argument about it between Charlotte and Alice. I suppose with Alice having helped me with Harry's girls when they were all little, she felt they should go to her. She could have squeezed them all in, but she only had the one spare room and only a yard at the back of the shop. Ernest and Charlotte have a nice big house with three bedrooms and a long back garden that goes down to the river, so they had more space. It didn't matter in the end as Emily said the girls would stay at Alpine Street.

Alice still took the girls and sometimes Vi and James to St Giles every Sunday. Bert wasn't much of a religious man, but Alice took it very seriously. She said it gave her comfort, and strength when David went missing. Ernest, Charlotte and Josie would go as well, so the girls could see their cousin. Emily would go back to Alpine Street straight after the service to take over with Vi and James, but Kitty and Lily often went to Ernest and Charlotte's for their Sunday lunch. Granny North would get out sometimes, and the girls would find her wandering down the road and have to take her back indoors again. I hope I never end up like Granny North, not knowing if it was raining or Wednesday.

I must say, time has passed much faster since I've been in London. When I think back to my own girlhood, back in West Court, and then with Watmore in Bedford Court, it seems like a very long time ago. But it only feels like five minutes ago that I woke up in that church in Paddington and counted out my coppers on that wooden pew.

I wasn't badly off at the boarding house in Kingsland but it could be noisy, especially at the weekends with doors banging at all hours. I was saving a bit each week, and I started looking for somewhere a bit quieter. I saw a card in the post office window one day saying a lady wanted a companion to cook and do a bit of light cleaning in exchange for a room in her house. The address was in Haggerston, so I went and had a look. The house was in St Nicholas Square. It was much grander than anything in Kingsland. I'd already made up my mind that if the woman was as mad as Granny North then it wouldn't matter how nice the room or house was, I wouldn't take it on. I didn't want to be anyone's nursemaid, but I could do a bit of cooking and cleaning and have a chat during the day.

Mrs Boyd was very nice. She showed me into her front parlour and I could tell she was of good breeding, just like the sisters in Caversham had been. She reminded me a lot of them, and I suppose if she had had a sister then she might not have wanted a companion. Mrs Boyd was a widow and her son, Peter, lived on the other side of London. He was something in the City, a lawyer or some-such. Peter would visit every other week on a Thursday afternoon for tea, and sometimes he would take Mrs Boyd out for an hour or two if the weather was nice.

She wasn't at all like Granny North and that was a relief to me. Mrs Boyd was what young people call 'spritely' these days, and she was only 15 years older than me. We could have been sisters ourselves. She went to the church on the corner, St Chad's that one was, and to the library and the shops. She had two or three friends who would come to tea now and then. She said she really just wanted to know that someone else was in the house in the evenings and not to have to cook and clean for herself. She said that was why she didn't want a younger girl, because they'd be out in the evenings dancing or what have you. Well, we hit it off together straight away.

She showed me the kitchen, lovely big room it was with a gas oven and pots and pans you could see your face in. There was a big copper for the laundry and plenty of soap in the scullery. Then she showed me what would be my own room, and the bathroom between her room and mine. The lav was in a separate little room at the other end of the landing, and there was another one next to the scullery. Two lavs, both indoors! I'd never seen such luxury. We came to an agreement over wages and duties and such, and I moved my things in at the end of that week.

I didn't miss the walk to the munitions factory, I can tell you that much. Mrs Boyd had her ways as you'd expect, and she liked things just so, but we soon fell in together and I had such a nice time working for her. It didn't take a lot to keep the place clean once I'd got my routine sorted out. Cooking was straight forward for the two of us. Mrs Boyd would tell me at breakfast what she fancied for her dinner, and I'd go out to the High Street and get whatever it was. Lunch was a sandwich or omelette, just something light. Then Mrs Boyd would have a lie down for an hour or so and I could go out or do whatever I pleased before it was time to start tea. Yes, we got along together very well.

I was with Mrs Boyd when we started to hear of people getting very sick with the influenza in 1918. She came back from church one day and said how the congregation was only half the usual size as so many were ill. She was rather worried about it all, and when Peter came later that week, he said she was to stay at home as much as possible and not see anyone. Mrs Boyd wasn't happy about that, I can tell you. It was getting on for her birthday at the start of August and she'd already been planning a party with her friends. I had a long list of cakes and puddings to make and extra provisions to find down the High Street. That wasn't easy either, what with the war on and some food being scarce or if it was there, it was two or three times the price it had been before. We were going to have a table and chairs out in the back garden if the weather stayed nice, with the best china and glassware.

Then one of Mrs Boyd's friends caught it and was dead within a week. That shocked her. It shocked me too, if truth be told. I'd been getting to know Mrs Boyd's friends and they were all lovely old ladies. No trouble to anyone and always asking after my health. Now it was their health that was the worry. There were notices in the newspapers about keeping windows open and to stay away from crowds. That was easier said than done; we had to eat! But it was quieter in the High Street, I did notice that, especially as we got to Mrs Boyd's birthday. Only two of her friends came out of the fifteen that were invited, and she was so very upset by it all, but she put on a brave face, and I think they had a jolly nice time of it in the end. We still put the table in the garden with some of her own flowers in a big vase in the middle.

It seemed like the influenza was going away towards the end of the summer that year. Peter suggested that Mrs Boyd have another party to make up for her friends not being able to go to the first one. We had that one indoors in the parlour on account of it being a wet evening on the date she'd chosen. I was dog tired after that night! We got a young girl in to help me serve at the table but everything else was down to me and I didn't get to bed until gone two the next morning. Mrs Boyd was very kind. She gave me an extra half a crown for myself in the housekeeping the next week to thank me for making everything go so well for her and her friends. I told her I enjoyed it, but I was thankful for the extra and I bought myself a new pair of stockings and some barley sugar twists and put the rest away.

A few days later Mrs Boyd didn't get up for her breakfast when she usually did. I knocked on her bedroom door with a tray about seven, and she was still in her bed but soaked through with sweat. Poor dear could hardly speak and then later that day she started coughing. Oh that sound, I shall never forget it. It took every ounce of strength from her, that cough did. Day and night, it's a wonder I never came down with it myself, looking after her as I was. I thought she was done for when she started coughing up blood, I really did. Peter sent for the doctor, though they were so busy with everyone else being so ill at the same time. It took three days before a doctor came and by then Mrs Boyd seemed to be on the mend. He gave me instructions to boil all of the bedding, her nightclothes and the handkerchiefs, as if I needed telling!

It took her ever such a long time to get better. She was never really her old self again, though she still went to church regularly. I'd never wanted to be a nursemaid, as I said before, after seeing to Granny North, so I was in a bit of a bind with Mrs Boyd. Peter wanted me to stay on, and he gave me a bit of extra money each week for my trouble.

If I left Mrs Boyd, I'd have to find somewhere else to live too, and that house was all I could wish for at my time of life. Peter must have read my mind, because one day after he'd been to see his mother, he came into the kitchen to speak to me. He said how grateful he was that I'd been there to help Mrs Boyd but as she wasn't as strong as she had been he was thinking of getting in a real nurse to care for her. I thought my number was up! But then he said that he would still want me to stay and cook and clean as I had been, but that he would rather have a professional nurse in to do that side of things. So, I stayed.

I wrote to Alice about it, to see how things were in Reading. She told me little Josie had died of it. That was no surprise, the girl had been sickly all her short life. Johnny had been ill with it but survived, as had Louisa and the children although George was spared. He said it was down to him being out of doors all day. Alice said there were reports in the newspaper of people dropping down dead in the middle of Broad Street. We heard that in Hackney as well, and of others being put out of their homes when they couldn't pay the rent on account of being too ill to work. They had to open the Town Hall up for people to go and claim some relief from the parish it was that bad. And they couldn't bury the bodies fast enough.

Fred wrote to say that his pals were all dropping like flies from it in France, but that he was keeping well and hoped to be coming back to London soon. He said other things too but a lot of it was blacked out so I couldn't read it. I was glad to hear he was alright, even so.

Yes, so I stayed on with Mrs Boyd until the spring of 1921. Now, I can't meet you next week, I've got other appointments. So shall we say two weeks from now, but perhaps closer to eleven?

Laura has more questions

As Laura pulled the final sheet of paper from the typewriter and placed it onto the pile on the table, her mind was full of confusion. Two things principally pulled at her from all angles. First, all that she had been assured of by Lucy Worthington, that a woman would fight tooth and nail to keep her children by her side, had been thrown to the four winds by Mrs Hawkins' revelation that she had deliberately left all of her children behind. Second, the warning Mrs Hawkins had given Laura not to fully trust what her 'young man' said in relation to any extra dalliances he might be involved in. It troubled Laura greatly.

On the second point, Laura was now officially engaged to Clive and the wedding date had been set for the following April. A spring wedding followed by a short honeymoon in Dorset seemed, on the face of it, a simple thing to agree to. However, Laura had become aware that at parties and dinners when she accompanied Clive, there had been a circle of other young women to whom Clive paid almost equal attention. They touched his hand, they kissed his cheek; he bought them drinks and offered cigarettes with abandon. Was there more to Clive's actions than a friendliness and need to impress the right people?

Laura would not say that she loved Clive. She liked him very much, she enjoyed his company and felt the two of them understood each other. But if she was to become Mrs Laura Merton, Mrs Hawkins' remarks persuaded her that she needed some kind of assurance from Clive that she was the only woman in his life (besides his mother, sister and cousins, naturally). Laura resolved to broach the subject with Clive the following Sunday when they were to take a drive into the Oxfordshire countryside. At the risk of being stranded should Clive take offence, Laura did not want to put the discussion off now that the seeds of doubt had been sown.

The first point of concern which centred on Mrs Hawkins' abandonment of her children troubled Laura more than Clive's potential for affairs. Laura had felt she was beginning to understand the older woman as being someone to whom life happened without much influence on Mrs Hawkins' part. Laura had protested when Clive suggested that Mrs Hawkins – like so many others of her kind, he had said – was content to ride on the coat-tails of whatever man happened to show an interest in her. Laura pointed out the difficulties of finding employment when one had so many children to care for, to which Clive had replied again that having so many children was irresponsible if one could not provide for them. Laura felt strongly that it was not the fault of the Watmore, Jones and now North children that their parents were unable to provide fully and consistently for their well-being.

Mrs Hawkins was challenging Laura's concept of charity and how it was received by the poor. Laura had been brought up to think the poor would accept graciously, with perhaps a little token resistance, offers of assistance by well-meaning individuals who had the means to provide it. Reading back through her interviews, Laura picked out the instances where charity could have been available to Mrs Hawkins, yet she had either fallen back on her own community for support or had been alert enough to say the right things to the right people and achieve her goal. She had not sent her children away. She had not sent them to the workhouse. They had not been taken from her. Laura would have been less surprised had any of those three situations come to pass; it was what she had expected of a woman such as Mrs Hawkins.

Laura thought back at the lack of real emotion with which Mrs Hawkins had described her sister's death. Then there was the un-doubted shame she must have felt at becoming pregnant before her marriage to Watmore, of being complicit in the lie to enable her employment in Bermondsey, seeing her son sent away to a trade school, and then knowing they could not afford the rent on the Caversham house even as they agreed to take on the tenancy. If there had been shame felt, then Mrs Hawkins had long buried it, Laura decided. And why not? Was she really to blame for those things? There was a defiance in Mrs Hawkins that Laura felt had carried her through her trials and tribulations thus far. Laura wondered if she could learn from Mrs Hawkins, as well as gaining her journalism qualification.

As she replaced the cover over the typewriter, Laura considered how she might behave if she ever found herself in a similar situation to Mrs Hawkins. Stealing an apple or pear from a market stall: no, that would surely never occur. Falling pregnant out of wedlock: also highly unlikely given that Laura was still a virgin and intended to remain so until Clive's wedding ring was securely on her finger. Having too many children: but how many would be too many for Laura and Clive? Laura was aware of the strategies a woman, or a couple, could employ to avoid having children if they wished. Clive would be away from home more often as his career developed and Laura would have the option of either staying in England (presumably to raise a family) or to accompany him to whatever country needed his attention.

The idea suddenly occurred to Laura that were she to remain at home with a growing gaggle of babies, she would be emulating Mrs Hawkins and the temptation to run away later on would become a distinct possibility. Despite their vastly different beginnings in life, Laura could find herself faced with the same decisions that Mrs Hawkins had had to make. Perhaps the answer would be to have no children, so that the decision would never have to be made.

Which brought Laura back to Mrs Hawkins' warning about men and their ways. Twice at least Mrs Hawkins had been set aside for another woman by the man she thought of as her own. The revelation that Thomasina was the product of such an action, and with her then best friend no less, must surely have been devastating had Mrs Hawkins discovered it sooner. Laura wondered if Mrs Hawkins would have thrown Watmore out. Would she have had a blazing row with Minnie Draper in the middle of the court? Or would she have simply accepted it all and focused on her own children? She had hinted that she suspected Watmore of affairs, but if he continued to return home then those could perhaps be ignored. Thomasina was living proof which would have been almost impossible to ignore, though, Laura realised, Watmore could have denied his part in her conception.

Laura would have liked to interview Minnie Draper, to find out her side of the story. Yet she knew that was both unnecessary for her assignment and a betrayal of the trust she had established with Mrs Hawkins. Instinctively she understood that Minnie's willingness to help Mrs Hawkins through the two births and beyond was her way of saying sorry to her friend for the betrayal with Watmore. What tangled lives these people led!

One thing was certain in Laura's mind: she needed to know the final instalment of Mrs Hawkins' life story, if only to avoid any similar catastrophes in her own.

Interview 6.

[I sensed that we were nearing the end of Mrs Hawkins'
tale and so agreed to meet her for lunch again at my own
expense. We had reached 1921 and I was keen to understand
how she had dealt with having to move on again as she
entered her fifth decade. L.C.]

P eter Boyd was very good to me, you know, and he needn't have
   been. Some women get turned out the moment their mistress is
in the ground without a by your leave. I was very lucky to have met
him and his mother when I did, I know that much. He said he was
going to put the house up for rent, but that he would give me a month
to find somewhere else, and pay me two months as severance. You see,
he was a very kind man. The nurse, Ruth, didn't live in. She'd come
daily from Shoreditch, so she just got her severance from Peter. I liked
Ruth, but she could be a bit above herself sometimes, especially if she
thought the linen wasn't boiled long enough. I don't think she'd ever

had to boil linen in her life, so I held my tongue when she went on about it.

Anyway, there I was with no job and nowhere to live again. Fred was back from the war and living in Pimlico, but I knew he wouldn't want his old mum living with him. He was going up in the world, going into politics. He did say he would help me out with rent though, if I needed a few shillings extra a week. I could have gone to Alice, but I could tell by her letters that she was still cut up rough over David and I didn't want to be stuck with her sobbing all day. I would have been too close to Alpine Street for comfort as well, so that really wasn't a good idea.

Emily had started her teacher training by then. She was still living in Alpine Street, but she went every day to the college. I do think if Lily hadn't married Ron, then all three of Harry's girls would have stayed together.

I went to see Minnie and Frank, not to ask them to take me in, but to see if they knew of any cheap lodgings. Of course, they did say that I was welcome to go in with them if I couldn't find somewhere else, but they had done so much for me already. Mind you, it was good to know I wouldn't be out on the streets if it came to it! Times were hard back then. What with all the soldiers coming home and wanting their jobs, and the young girls not wanting to give them up. And it's not as if they could marry and live like we used to; there weren't enough young men to go round, and those who came home weren't always in one piece. Some men got angry about it all. There were riots at some of the factories with the men demanding that the women be sacked. The munitions factory closed of course, and that put more young women out of work. I didn't think I'd be able to find anything more than a bit of cleaning and that wouldn't be enough for more than a room in a boarding house again.

I was feeling a bit down in the dumps about it all and I had about a week left before I had to leave Mrs Boyd's house. I went down to the church and had a look on their notice board, and I could hear the organist inside practicing, so I went in to have a listen for a while. I was sitting there minding my own business when Archie Bennet came in. He was one of the church wardens and he'd come to have a look at the electrics, on account of him being an electrician. We'd known each other since I went to Mrs Boyd's, and we'd laughed at how we shared the same birthday, date and year. He lost his mother with the influenza, and he'd never married.

We got chatting while the organist was playing and before I knew it, I'd told him of my situation. He rubbed his chin in that way he had, and then said that he had two empty rooms in his house and would I consider them. I said to him, Archie Bennet, are you propositioning me? I said, I'm too old for any funny business! He was quiet for a moment and then he said if I'd feel better about it, we could get married and do it all proper, but that I could still have his two spare rooms. He was used to having a woman about the place he said, and knowing I was a widow, he'd been thinking of asking me for a while. Well, I never had any idea about that!

We talked it all over, sat there on a pew in St Chad's and when the organist finished his practice we'd agreed to go and see the vicar straight away. I can see by your face that you think I was being rash. You girls have things so much easier these days. Archie was a good man. Once we'd spoken to the vicar – who was very happy for us, I must say – I went to have a look at Archie's house. It wasn't the size of Mrs Boyd's of course, no front garden and just a yard at the back, but Archie had kept it nice and tidy, and the two rooms upstairs were clean.

I explained everything to Peter, and when he heard I'd be getting married in three weeks he said I could stay until then. He hadn't found anyone new to rent the house yet, so he was happy to have someone minding it still for him. That was a weight off my mind. I invited him to the wedding, but he was busy at his job and couldn't come. He did send us a lovely set of cutlery though, in one of those boxes with a satin lining and a little clasp on the front. Such a kind man.

It wasn't a large affair. Fred came to give me away, which was good of him. Archie had one of the other church wardens, Benny Tobin as his best man. Minnie and Frank and the girls came, and one or two others from the church but that was all. We didn't want anything flashy you see, we just wanted to do it properly and not have everyone gossiping. Archie had a small disablement pension from the army as he'd joined up at the start of the war and got shot in the leg just above his ankle almost as soon as he put his uniform on. He used to joke about it, but I know he felt ashamed that he hadn't been able to do his bit. He hadn't had to go off to the Front, he did it because he thought it was the right thing to do. I did a bit of cleaning at the Co-Op offices every morning, and we managed on what we had.

Archie was true to his word. There was no funny business between us. He put a lick of paint around the smallest of the two rooms for me and I had it like a little parlour with a table in the window and an armchair by the fireplace. I got into the habit of making his meals when I did mine. It was no extra trouble, and I was used to cooking for two. He liked us to go to church together every Sunday. I wasn't keen, but it kept him happy, and it was no skin off my nose to do it, so I did.

All that time I thought that house was rented. I used to say to him when he was painting this or fixing that, why make so much effort when it belongs to someone else? And he'd just shrug and smile and say we'd benefit from it too. I had no idea that it belonged to Archie until he died last year. I know some of the women at church don't believe that, but I swear on my Fred's good name it's true. Archie had made a will – I didn't even know that until I got the solicitor's letter. He had no one else to leave any of it to, you see.

I took the letter over to Minnie and Frank because I couldn't make head nor tail of all the fancy words in it. Frank had a look and said Archie had left me everything: the house, and a share in a boat yard down at the Royal canal. He'd never mentioned that either, though it turned out he'd got the shares from his father years ago. Frank also said that as Archie's dependent, I could apply for a war widow's pension, on account of Archie being discharged from the army with his ankle.

I sat there dumbfounded in their back room. I couldn't take it all in. I wouldn't have to work, and I'd be able to stay in our little house for as long as I needed to. Archie had been my knight in shining armour as they say. He'd stepped in when I was almost down and out, and he'd left me well provided for. And do you know, I felt I'd earned it too. All those years looking after everyone else, all the meals I missed just to make sure the children had something to eat, all the times I'd hidden from the rent man or had to pinch a few lumps of coal to keep warm. I might not have made much of myself, but I'd come out on top for once.

I suppose I should see about making a will too, now that I've got something to leave behind. Gawd knows how much the children would get, having nine to share it. I shall ask Fred about it next time I see him. He's away at the moment, some party business he said in Manchester of all places.

The rest? They're all pretty much as they've been all along. Alice is still in London Street with Johnny in the shop. George and Louisa and the children are over at Newtown and he's a manager now at Suttons. Ernest and Charlotte haven't had any more children, but they're still in Elgar Road. Ernest still rides his motorcycle to the pig farm and back every day. Emily passed her exams and is a teacher where they all went to school at George Palmer's on Whitley Street. I'm sure I told you, Kitty lives with Emily on Northumberland Avenue behind the school and she's got a good job at the telephone exchange. Lily worked at Wantage Hall at the University for a while, then she married Ron a couple of years ago and Emily says she had a baby boy, Daniel. Vi and James are still with Bert. Emily has Vi in her class at the school.

So, is that everything you wanted to know? How long will it take you to type all those notes up? Well good luck with your course, dear. It's been very nice chatting with you these past few weeks. Say hello to Lucy for me if you see her before I do, We don't keep in touch as often as we used to these days, even with the telephones. And you have a word with your young man.

Laura's resolve

After she paid for their lunch, Laura left the café and walked in the late autumn sunshine towards the station. Leaves crunched beneath her feet and rearranged themselves against the bases of trees and hedges in the breeze. Hackney was bustling, and children could be heard playing in a school yard as the bell sounded to call them back to their studies. Laura was acutely aware of every individual she passed. A thousand questions about each one ran through her mind. Her mother would have chastised her for being nosy, had Mrs Curtly known. It wasn't nosiness, Laura told herself, it was her investigative nature. What a splendid woman police constable she would have made!

Her concerns about Clive's potential other women had been allayed. Their drive into Oxfordshire had, with hindsight, not been the best time to bring up the subject. Laura had wanted to get it off her chest as quickly as possible having stewed over the situation for long enough, and had asked Clive bluntly as they passed Taplow if he was seeing anyone else. He turned his head to stare at Laura with incredulity and narrowly missed a tractor which was heading in the opposite direction. He had not answered, being preoccupied with swearing at the tractor, and Laura had not pressed him to at that moment. Later, when they had unpacked a picnic by the side of the Thames at Wallingford, Clive handed Laura a packet of corned beef sandwiches.

"Why did you ask me if I was seeing someone else earlier?"

Laura looked from the sandwiches to Clive's face. "Because I wanted to be sure."

"It's that Hawkins woman again, isn't it?"

"Not exactly. Partly. I was thinking about how she had been betrayed by her first husband, Watmore, and then her third, Mr North. She took it all rather well, except for screaming at North's fancy woman in the street. I had been thinking how I might behave if I found out that you were unfaithful."

"You are a strange bird, Laura. I can't imagine you screaming at anyone in the street and would hope never to witness it. Mrs Hawkins must have a jolly low opinion of men if that's how she has been treated."

"Actually no, she doesn't. You see, that's the last piece of her story. The lady she had been companion to died, and while Mrs Hawkins was looking for somewhere else to live, one of the church wardens proposed to her."

"That would be husband number ... four?"

"Yes! It got her out of a bind, but what she didn't know – she says – is that Archie Bennet owned his own house and had some shares in a boat yard. He died just a little while ago and left everything to Mrs Hawkins."

"Well I never. So, she's finally come up smelling of roses? Good for Mrs Hawkins. But hold on a moment, if she was still married to the North fellow, and then married the chap in London, that's bigamy!

That's illegal you know. Laura, really, I think she should be reported to the police."

The situation had not occurred to Laura, despite hearing it from Mrs Hawkins and then reading it as she typed up her notes later. Of course, it was bigamy, though strangely it was usually men that one read about in the newspapers who committed that particular crime.

"I hadn't realised, but yes I suppose you are right. I don't see any benefit in reporting her now though, not now that Archie Bennet has died too. According to Mrs Hawkins there were no other relations for Archie to leave his worldly possessions to."

"It's still a crime, and more so if she has benefitted from it materially, I should say."

Laura considered it all for a moment before answering.

"There might have been a time when I would have agreed with you completely. But now, well yes she has benefitted, but what benefit would there be of prosecuting her? Who would benefit then? If it all came out, her children and grandchildren would all be embarrassed by it, don't you think? I shan't be seeing her again. I think we should let sleeping dogs lie. Promise me you won't mention it to anyone?"

"I suppose there's no real harm done there. The woman's life sounds like a bally mess if you ask me. I'm glad it's all over with - perhaps now she will stop putting these fanciful ideas into your head!" Clive cut himself a slice of pork pie and took a bite.

"Darling, that's not what she has been doing. But you didn't answer me when I asked you earlier."

"I was trying to avoid killing us both. Do you really need an answer? Will you believe me? These kinds of questions always feel like a double jeopardy, and I must say I find it all very distasteful having my honour called into doubt, particularly on the instigation of a bigamist."

Laura bit her lip. For all his intelligence and ability, Clive could often be an idiot. He was no use with a motor engine and didn't know lupins from lavender. His career would depend upon his ability to be economical with the truth, to advance one theory or proposal over others that might be less beneficial to his adversaries without giving the game away. Clive would make a dedicated and successful diplomat, she was certain. And even if there were other women, he was there with her on the banks of the Thames, sharing a pork pie in the last of the autumn sunshine.

"Do you want a family one day, children?" She asked.

Clive swallowed the last of his slice of pie and dabbed his mouth with a napkin before wiping grease from his fingers. "I have a feeling that whatever I say will be the wrong answer. Do you?"

"Clive, I don't want us to start off on the wrong foot and do things just because they are expected of us. I do intend to be your wife, and as far as I'm concerned that commitment is for life. But hearing Mrs Hawkins story ..."

Clive threw up his hands in exasperation, "That woman!"

"Yes, that woman as you describe her, that woman who has really lived and survived and is now doing well for herself, has opened my eyes to situations I had never and probably would not ever have considered. My mind feels wider, expanded, and I understand now that there are certain expectations of married women that I might not be able to live up to."

"You mean to continue with this ... journalism? Even once we are married?"

"I should like to do something, though it might not come to an engagement with a newspaper. With your job, I should think having a journalist as a wife could be an impediment to open conversation. But

I could write articles for magazines. Perhaps even write a book after all. Mother would like that at least."

"Your shorthand could come in handy I suppose. But now it's you who is avoiding the question."

Laura glanced across the river. She had more opportunities than Mrs Hawkins, but even so, children would close those doors to her as if they had never been opened. She had a desire to wade into the river and let it carry her back to London, out into the north sea and beyond.

"I think ... I'd rather not."

Clive let go of the breath he had been holding and reached for Laura's hand. "I think I'd rather not as well. Even though we'll be able to afford them, I should hardly see them from one month to the next and I was rather hoping that you would want to come with me when I'm posted abroad."

"You don't want to buy a house somewhere out of the city? Somewhere like this?"

"Not unless it's what you want. My apartment is large enough for the two of us, and so convenient for town. If you are certain you don't want children, there's no need to find anywhere larger."

"And you really do want me to travel with you?"

"Wherever it's possible, of course I do. The gossip in Whitehall is that things are hotting up on the continent, and I wouldn't want you following me into anywhere that was dangerous. If you're with me, I shan't have the worry of some gardener or handyman sweeping you off your feet and away from me." Clive attempted a smile, but Laura saw the frown and was touched by Clive's vulnerability.

"No children, then. Mother will be terribly disappointed, and I'm sure yours will be too. Do you think we should keep our decision just between us?"

"Yes. Perhaps I can find you a position in the Diplomatic Corps as well!"

Epilogue

I t had been a long drive. Far longer than Michael's usual trips around Norfolk on business, it had been enough to convince him to trade up to a new Ford Granada while he could still get a good price for the Cortina. Michael pulled into the parking space on the third floor of the Chatham Street car park in Reading, thankful for their comfort stop just outside of St Albans an hour and a half earlier. Beside him sat Lisa, his eldest daughter, holding the box of papers that were destined for the museum archivist.

While Michael would have been happy to make the drive alone, he had no complaints about Lisa accompanying him. She had taken far more interest in his mission than his wife Evelyn. Lisa even suggested they combine the trip with a visit to the University so that she might get a feel for the place before making her final decision on where to continue her studies.

"We're still a bit early. Are you hungry?" Michael asked as he sifted through the coins from his pocket to feed into the ticket machine.

"Not really. I could do with a drink though. I wonder if they have a Wimpy here." Lisa rested the box on the roof of the Cortina.

"We can have a look. We've got to walk through the town to get to the museum." Michael called over his shoulder on his way to pay for their parking space.

With Michael carrying the box, they made their way out of the concrete car park and past the curious flint façade of the Greyfriars church that stood sentinel at the beginning of Friar Street. Glancing along West Street, Lisa spotted a familiar red-and-white Wimpy sign and led her father past the long Co-Operative windows before crossing the street and entering the narrow burger restaurant. Michael was unsurprised when Lisa changed her mind and asked for a bean burger and fries along with her drink. Having made do with coffee in St Albans, Michael ordered a cooked breakfast with tea and checked with the waitress that the museum was at the other end of Friar Street.

While Lisa was using the toilet at the rear of the restaurant, Michael let his mind wander to consider a possible choice of Reading as her university. He was proud of her dedication to her studies; she was expected to do well in her A-levels having picked up a couple of AS-levels the previous summer. She excelled in English and history, and despite a careers interview where she was encouraged to take a science or language, had picked Art as her third option. How different she was to her sister Karen, younger by two years and about to sit her mock O-levels. Karen had always been sporty, which Michael and Evelyn had encouraged with swimming lessons, horse riding, cycling and tennis alongside the netball and hockey that the school provided. Karen had no interest in A-levels, despite Michael's regular attempts to change her mind. She had already started a Saturday job at the leisure centre with her sights set on becoming a lifeguard.

And then there was Paul. Michael would never admit it, but his cup of pride overflowed when he thought of his son and the potential he was already showing. Next year he would move from Prep to the Senior School and would be able to take advantage of the extra-curricular activities that the older boys enjoyed. Paul's technical drawing skills were excellent, as were his abilities in art and languages, and he was a keen wicket keeper. Michael had high hopes for him and did not begrudge a moment of weekend working to pay the school fees. Laura's bequest would go a long way to reducing those hours in the future.

The waitress brought the drinks to the Formica-topped table and Michael moved the box onto the seat next to his own. Despite not having children of her own, Laura had always shown a genuine interest in her nieces and nephews. Three years earlier they had spent a family holiday together in Aldeburgh on the Suffolk coast, and Lisa in particular had taken to her great aunt as if they had been old friends. That had been just before Clive's death, and Michael suddenly felt ashamed that he had not seen his aunt since Clive's funeral.

"Why so glum, chum?" Lisa asked as she returned to the table.

"I was remembering your great aunt and uncle, and the holiday we had together just before uncle Clive died."

"In Suffolk? I remember. Auntie Laura had so many stories. I wish we'd known about her papers then; I could have read them all."

"Would you really have wanted to?"

"Of course! It's history, dad. It's my thing you know." She looked towards the approaching waitress, "oh great, I'm starving!"

They ate in silence, the restaurant almost empty save for a woman at a window table nursing a cup of coffee and smoking a long cigarette. Michael wondered if Lisa had tried a cigarette; he thought she probably had. Laura had smoked, as did many of her generation. Had

Mrs Hawkins? No, he remembered her comment about the other girls smoking out of the windows in the interview transcripts.

"I wonder what would have been here in Mrs Hawkins' day." Lisa broke into his thoughts. "Do you think it was very different to now?"

"I don't know, I've only been here once before, on the way to visit Laura and Clive years ago, and then only briefly. I remember the town centre having very tall red-brick buildings."

"I should have liked to see the courts that Mrs Hawkins grew up in."

"Why ever would you want to do that?" Michael turned up his nose at the thought.

"To see if they really were as awful as she described them. If she had such a bad start in life, she was pretty lucky to end it owning a house in London and some shares in a boatyard, don't you think? I wonder what happened to all of her children."

"Laura doesn't seem to have kept in touch after the end of the interviews. She and Clive moved to Paris soon after they married. I expect Mrs Hawkins' children might still be living around Reading. They would have been a similar age to Laura."

"I suppose they must be. We might walk right past one of them today and not realise. Do you think Mrs Hawkins would have gone to university if she hadn't met that Watmore character?"

Michael swallowed a mouthful of bacon. They had both read through the interviews a few times, along with some of the others Laura had conducted. Mrs Hawkins had emerged as one of the more interesting characters, even as Laura's narrative skills improved with each new individual.

"I doubt it. Not that she wasn't intelligent, but I think she would have eventually met someone else, married, had a family. That's what women like that did back then."

"Auntie Laura didn't go to university either did she."

"No, although women could by then. It wasn't really seen as necessary. She bucked convention by not having children, though it was probably just as well she didn't what with all the travelling they did."

"She told me she wanted to be a policewoman but everyone said she couldn't."

"Really? I never knew that. It doesn't surprise me though. Laura was always a bit of an eccentric."

Michael chose not to tell Lisa how his mother had so often talked disparagingly about Laura. She had been critical of every change of residence, every Christmas card received from a far-away land, and in particular grasped every opportunity to announce that Laura wasn't 'natural' for not wanting children. Selfish was the other word so often aimed at Laura in her absence. Michael's sister Lucinda had picked up the thread of their mother's incredulity early on, though with less regularity in expressing her similar feelings. In Lucinda's mind, women were meant to be maternal, to actively want children and to sacrifice whatever personal interests they may have in order for their offspring to have 'what we never had'. Michael tried to think what Lucinda had wanted to be when they were growing up, but in his mind's eye he only ever remembered her playing with her dolls and arranging tea parties for them in the back garden of their farmhouse.

From what he'd known, seen, and more recently read about Laura's life, he didn't think she had missed out on anything by not having children. Quite the contrary; she had always appeared to relish the life she and Clive had embarked on together. Michael wondered how much Mrs Hawkins had influenced his aunt, and how much she might have influenced Lisa had the two ever met.

They handed over the box of papers to a very appreciative, if softly-spoken archivist at the museum. Lisa was keen to look round the

exhibitions while she had the opportunity, particularly the old photographs of the town enlarged to fill panels on the walls of one room
to tell the story of Reading from the Middle Ages onwards. Michael
chatted to the archivist. He learned that some of the locations mentioned in the interviews still existed, and as he and Lisa were going on
to the University the archivist explained that it wasn't so very far from
there to St Giles and Whitley. She gave Michael a small, folded street
map of the town on which she marked the locations that Michael
was able to remember. When Lisa reappeared, the archivist wished her
good luck with her studies and suggested that if Lisa were to choose
Reading to study at, she would be welcome to visit the archives again.

The town centre was growing busy with shoppers and workers
from the offices above many of the shops. Processions of double-deck-
er busses rumbled up and down Broad Street. Michael had been
correct about the red-brick architecture. Father and daughter made
their way to Redlands behind the Royal Berkshire Hospital to the
London Road campus of the University. More red brick, yet here was
an oasis of green in the bustling town. One of the porters showed them
around the courtyard, pointing out where the various departments
had rooms. Then he suggested they visit the residential halls, either
Mansfield or Wantage, if Lisa was thinking of studying there. Lisa was
impressed with the feel of the campus, the friendliness of the porter
and the students in their colourful clothes and with books and folders
clutched to their chests as they crossed the lawns.

Leaving the University campus and following the map which
Michael continually pulled from his pocket, checked, pointed at a
landmark and refolded, they made their way towards Silver Street. Lisa
had wanted to see the apartments that Mrs Hawkins had crammed her
growing family into before her marriage to Albert North. As the pair
stood at the edge of the small square, Lisa let out a low whistle.

"They're just bedsits, aren't they? I mean, the washing lines are right, they must have been here forever, but how could you get six children in one of those?"

"They probably weren't designed to hold that many, but I've no doubt that they did. Overcrowding isn't a new thing."

"What was yours and Mum's first house like?"

"We had a flat just off King's Lynn High Street. It wasn't much larger than these really, but when your mother knew she was going to have you, we bought the house we have now. We wanted somewhere with plenty of space."

"Mrs Hawkins must have been a strong woman to manage so many children in such a small home. And then she moved just a couple of streets away? Can we go there?"

Michael looked at his watch. "Alright, but then we need to get back to the car."

They found Alpine Street easily and tried to guess exactly which house had been Mrs Hawkins' home. Lisa pointed down the steep street towards Elgar Road and reminded Michael that Ernest and his little family had lived there.

"They feel real, don't you think? Now that we've been to the places that they knew, it's almost as if I can feel them watching us. I think that's why I like history so much, Dad, there are so many interesting people to find out about."

"I think that's how your Auntie Laura felt. She was just interested in people. She once told me that she learned something new from every person she spoke to."

"And she visited here too, didn't she. It was in her notes, she came to see if she could ... what's the word..."

"Corroborate?"

"Yes! To see if what Mrs Hawkins had told her was true. And now we're doing almost the same thing, aren't we."

"They do say that history repeats itself."

Lisa put her hand through his arm as they turned back towards Southampton Street. "They offer journalism at Reading as well as history. Perhaps I could do both."

Michael smiled down at his daughter. "Perhaps you'll meet a budding diplomat too."

Author's note

As writers, we naturally take inspiration from everything we see and hear around us, and from our own experiences and family circumstances. There is nothing new under the sun, as my own mother used to regularly say!

The characters in this work are fictional in as much as there is no individual that I am aware of who has experienced the exact same timeline of events as either Laura or Mrs Hawkins. However, many (though not all) of the events in Mrs Hawkins' life story do have a few toes in reality, if not a whole foot. My great grandmother is the basis for some of those events. She was, I believe, a formidable woman, a secretive woman, and a woman who like Mrs Hawkins was 'married' at least three times and had eleven or possibly twelve children. Records are unfortunately difficult to match up, and so this work of fiction can in no way be said to be her life story. I have also borrowed events from other relatives in my family tree, some going back over two centuries, and all now passed on.

With Laura's character, I wanted a means of tying Mrs Hawkins' experiences to the following generation without the complication or recriminations that another relative might bring. A young woman of good social standing in the 1930s would have had far more opportunities than Mrs Hawkins would ever have, though fewer still than Lisa who we meet at the end of the story. The contrast, I hope, has been successful.

While Laura and Mrs Hawkins meet each other in London, the places described in Reading are, or were, real locations around Reading in Berkshire. I invite you to visit and see how many you can find!

Mary Lay, 2023

Also by Mary Lay

The Catching Up series
Catching Up
The Price of Coal
Birds of the Storm
Equally Wrong (due 2024)

Short story collection
The Previous Adventures Of ...

If you enjoyed this novella, please leave a rating on Amazon or Goodreads!

Printed in Great Britain
by Amazon

27340204R00086